CRAVED BY THE ALIEN BEAST

BRIDES OF THE ZULDRUX WARRIORS, BOOK 1

AVA ROSS

ENCHANTED STAR PRESS

Craved by the Alien Beast

Brides of the Zuldrux Warriors, Book 1

Copyright © 2024 Ava Ross

All rights reserved.

Cover Art: Lunatic Covers

Editing: JA Wren and Owl Eyes Proofs & Edits

ALSO BY AVA ROSS

Find Ava's books on Amazon and her website,
avarosswrites(dot)com.

CRAVED BY THE ALIEN BEAST

I was stolen from Earth and gifted to an alien warrior. Will I find a new home with Aizor?

Vanessa: One minute, I'm working as a cook, the next, I've been abducted by robocops and sent to a distant planet where I'm attacked by a ferocious beast. Then a seven-foot-tall, blue-skinned alien rescues me with crystal spears slashing. He cuddles me in his arms, and I feel safe for the first time since fleeing my stalker ex.

Until he tosses me over his shoulder and takes me back to his clan where he announces I'm his new bride.

I'm determined to return home, but there's something about Aizor I can't resist. Am I falling for this muscle-bound alien with a killer smile?

Aizor: The crystal gods gifted me with Vanessa, and she's the prettiest being I've ever seen.

She's tiny.

Surprisingly snarly.

And she insists on returning to her home planet.

I have seven days to convince her to stay. I'll worship her. Massage her feet. And at night, I'll show her the gifts bestowed upon a Zuldrux warrior.

Then she'll accept she's my fated bride.

Craved by the Alien Beast is Book 1 of the Brides of the Zuldrux Warriors Series. Expect humor, size difference, devoted alien warriors who'll die to protect their fated mate, steamy romance, and a new alien world you'll want to live in.

Consent and HEA guaranteed.

Look for the rest of the Zuldrux Series!
Craved by the Alien Beast
Treasured by the Alien Rogue
Claimed by the Alien Barbarian
Cherished by the Alien Outlaw
Adored by the Alien Warlord

CHAPTER 1
VANESSA

My boss, Franklin, rushed into the kitchen of Dria's Diner where I worked.

"You've gotta come see this on TV," he said. "It's happening!"

After sliding the burger I'd just finished cooking from the grill and onto a bun, adding the requested toppings and a generous side of fries, I slid the plate onto the window between the kitchen and the guest area of the diner.

I tapped the bell. "Order's up."

A server hustled over to grab the plate while I followed Franklin into the dining area and looked up at the TV mounted in the corner. Guests had stopped eating and gazed as raptly as Franklin at the screen.

"It's about the upcoming launch," he said. "You don't want to miss *this*."

"They're sending a bunch of scientists to Mars in a

few weeks," one of the customers seated on a high-top at the bar said, his face glowing in the yellow lights humming above the island. He braced his forearms on the shiny counter. "What of it? I can't see why tonight's special."

"They're testing the propulsion systems," Franklin said. "If they work, the project's a go. They've been loading supplies in the hull for months. The crew will ride partway in stasis, then the rest of the time, they'll check out the view of the stars. Marvel at planets they pass. Get ready to start building the new colony on Mars. It's basically Star Trek come to life. How can you not be as into that as me?"

"Beam me up?" a woman quipped from beside the guy at the island, and they clinked their drinks together, laughing.

Franklin's shoulders deflated, but only for a moment before he shored them up again with his never-ending excitement. "You know what I mean. After the systems are ready, it's just a matter of fine-tuning everything else and loading the nonperishable food inside. It's gonna be *real*. We're going to settle some people on Mars and form our first colony. I tell ya, if I was younger," he stroked back his thinning gray hair, "and fitter. And smarter. Well, I'd be volunteering to be one of the first settlers."

"They're only going to send people with the right skills," the woman said. "I doubt running a diner is one of them."

"In the olden days, people like me ran inns for travelers." Franklin's chest puffed with pride. "Pubs like my diner were valued. Mark my words, there'll be inns in the new settlement eventually. Stores and movie theaters. Dance halls." He frowned. "Maybe dance halls. People love that kind of thing, and they want the colony to feel like home."

As much as it could feel that way on a planet far from Earth. I wasn't sure if I'd go even if I was offered a spot, which I wouldn't be. I liked having my feet planted firmly on the ground. Besides, I'd never meet the stringent criteria. I wasn't a rocket scientist, and I was curvy. Okay, I was extra curvy.

"I think the whole thing is cool," I said. Franklin was a good guy, and there was no harm in supporting his latest hobby. "Can you imagine what it will look like? A red planet. Craters. New dishes to create from the vegetation they'll grow within the hydroponic chambers." I rubbed my hands together at the thought.

I was taking classes at the community college, studying culinary arts. I wanted to be a chef. There was nothing wrong with working at the diner. I was grateful for the job. But I kept dreaming about opening my own restaurant, of crafting amazing dishes in a pristine kitchen for people who'd rave about the spices I used and the perfect way I'd prepared their meal.

It wouldn't be in outer space, but I was more than okay with that.

"There's great wealth on Mars," Franklin gushed,

warming to the subject. A few customers smiled, humoring him, but many nodded quite seriously. "All those new minerals. There must be gemstones and maybe even that planet's version of gold."

"I'm thinking of the plants and ways to test them to see if we can eat them," I said. "Someone could open up a restaurant there and serve all-Mars dishes."

Franklin nodded. "We could do it together."

Laughing, we high-fived each other.

After moving to Chicago, I could've done worse than land this job. Franklin had given me a chance and hadn't pressed hard when I told him I couldn't provide more than my driver's license for ID. On the run from a jerky ex, I'd left without much more than my coat and the wad of cash I'd stolen from his fireproof safe. I'd hopped on a bus and planned to hide for the rest of my life—or until my ex forgot I'd ever existed.

On the TV, the camera crew panned back from the ship perched on the launching platform, gliding across the AI robocops guarding the high, electrified fence. The odds of anyone getting past the cops were pretty much zero, and even if you somehow did, the fence would fry you to a crisp.

AI robocops had been introduced by a billionaire entrepreneur about a year ago, and they'd quickly taken over most of our city's police protection units. They might cost a boatload of money to buy, but they didn't need much maintenance, they could work 24/7, and they explicitly followed the law. No more cops going rogue and killing some kid with a toy pistol or complaining because they didn't want to work overtime.

Now they patrolled the streets of all the major cities, and crime had gone way down. Who'd challenge a robot who could outrun, outthink, and outsmart you before you could finish committing the crime? We all felt a bunch safer.

The show ended on the TV, cutting to a commercial.

Franklin was lifting the remote to turn it down, and I was heading back to the kitchen to prepare new orders when the front door of the diner slammed open.

Robocops poured in, their electronic, glowing red eyes sweeping across the room.

A red bead of light focused on my chest, and my hand froze on the door to the kitchen. I turned and backed against it, nearly falling into the room beyond.

The robocops whirred across the room, and as I scurried over to the wall beside the swinging door, two leaped over the counter. I gasped and lifted my hands, figuring they'd pass me and enter the kitchen. Like, maybe they wanted burgers. It was an inane thought, but it was all my frightened mind could come up with.

"Wait. What?" I yelped as the cops grabbed my arms, holding them tight enough to leave bruises. "I didn't do anything . . ."

Fuck, my ex had found me. I'd taken a chance using my driver's license to get this job and sign up for classes, thinking there was no way he could track me down, but it looked like he had.

Blubbering with fear and with my heart roaring up into my throat, I shrieked. My knees gave way.

I couldn't go back to him, couldn't let him throw me in jail.

One of the robocops poked my arm with something sharp, and the world swirled away . . .

AIZOR

"The hunt was good," I said to my fellow clan members, and they nodded. Many of my people sat on stumps, eating from crystal plates around the fire in the ceremonial chamber, a tall, blue and teal crystal structure that had once hosted my clan's god.

When it went silent, it took our future away with it.

My ancestors abandoned it, but I'd guided my clan back here not long ago. Now we couldn't imagine living anywhere else.

My gaze scanned the thirty males, four females, one of them elderly, plus our three precious young, only one of whom was female.

We few people were all that remained of my once thriving Indigan Clan. To think, when the crystals had been alive, there were so many Zuldruxians, thousands would attend the annual clan gatherings in the great valley below. Now we were lucky if a few hundred could make the trek to the event this coming season, the first to be held in years.

"Our hunters killed *three* bribards today," Jessia, one clan elder said, smacking her tusks. "We rarely see the like." She pushed her long braid of silver hair back over her shoulder. All of us shared the same hair color. "We'll smoke what's left tomorrow and store it for winter."

We'd all help. Ages ago, tasks had been divided between the sexes, but with so few females born to the remaining Zuldrux clans, duties that used to be exclusive to our females were divided among us all.

The bribard herds tended to cluster deep in the woods along the sides of the mountains during this season, making them a challenge to stalk. This hunt would feed my small clan for a long time, supplementing the food provided by our god.

The fire flared, highlighting the blue faces of those sitting closest to the warmth. Winter would be upon us soon, though we rarely saw snow in this part of the world.

The cold that came with the season was no longer a huge concern, unlike when we'd lived in rudimentary huts. Our god-given, crystal homes emitted heat, keeping us warm. In the hot months, they radiated cold, and it was common for us to remain inside, basking in the frigid air.

"Did you see any evidence of the Celedar Clan while hunting?" I asked Krute, my second-in-command.

He frowned into the flames. "Perhaps. Some crushed

vegetation on one of the trails. The persistent feeling of being watched."

I growled. The Celedar Clan lived in the forest between here and the central valley and their clan traedor, Nevarn, was determined to encroach on our land.

"Post more guards." He'd be foolish to attack my clan with so few males of his own, but a strong traedor protected the people he served.

Krute nodded and lifted his hand. Two males left our group and melted into the shadows beyond our crystal dwellings.

We finished our meal, complimenting the gods on the spices used on the tubers and the sauce one of the males had suggested for the grains. After, we placed our dishes inside a bin and one of the males carried it into the dining area in the back of the building where they would be absorbed and brought forth for our next meal.

I added more wood to the fire, noting how low the ceremonial pile had become. I'd already dropped numerous trees in early summer, and they would be dry enough by now to cut into smaller chunks and split.

Someone else *could* do it. After all, I was the clan leader and supposedly above menial tasks such as this, but I enjoyed the mindlessness of the activity. The work kept me strong and ready to do battle.

Assuming another clan attacked. Back when our clans were larger, fighting was common. Now, no clan wanted to lose even one member to prove they were stronger than the other.

"Gather round, little ones," Jessia said with a toothy

smile, settling back in the comfortable chair I'd crafted for her last winter. I'd cut the lumber, carefully sanding it down to ensure no splinter would pierce her thin skin and covered the finished product with soft cushions. "Sit, and I'll tell you the story of a world that once was, a world that now is, and a world that may yet wait for us."

A hush fell over those who hadn't left after the meal was finished. We'd all heard her tales numerous times, but each retelling felt fresh. It was good to remember, good to hear. Even better to believe that something would change to ensure that our world thrived once more.

Our two young boys left their indulgent parents and scurried around the fire to sit at Jessia's feet, gazing up at her raptly.

Willire nursed at her mother, Tepesta's breast, and was too young yet to listen.

Watching them, all of us sighed. Younglings were precious. They should be our future, but if our prayers were not answered soon, I didn't want to think of how things might be within five or even ten years.

My clan was dying and only the remaining gods could save us.

"No one knows when the crystal structures first planted themselves in the broad, open areas of our once glorious world," Jessia said in a lilting voice that drew all of us in.

Even the baby, Willire, looked toward her before returning to her mother's breast.

"Some say they arrived in silver ships and that they

descended from inside, walking stiffly down planks and out into the middle of the valley before sinking their roots deep within the soil," she said. "Others say the crystal structures were dropped from the ship, that they impaled the surface when they hit, driving spikes deep. Yet others suggest they've been here forever, even longer than our own people."

Muzzire, our strongest hunter, nodded. "I believe they've always been here. They're gods, after all, not beings from another world." He spat, the liquid sizzling in the fire, before nodding slowly. "Everything we will ever need is here on our planet."

Yet hope for something better might soon arrive from the stars.

Jessia grunted. She never enjoyed being interrupted. "In my story, we assume they descended from the stars. They are our gods, after all. However, it matters not if they were here always or came from somewhere else, does it?" A challenge rang out in her voice.

He said nothing, staring into the flames.

"Before the ships left, never to return, the varying structures were each infused with a god. The ships never returned, and our gods remained. We revered them, as we should, and they bestowed their goodness upon us." Her hand waved to the circle of glowing blue structures around us. "This . . . This crystal is still infused with a god."

Tepesta peered up while nursing her youngling, as if the god would reveal itself to us. Ours never did; not physically, that is. But we felt their presence in the way they cared for us, aided us. I'd brought my clan back to the Indigan lands three years ago, but it still felt like yesterday.

"What about our homes?" the youngest of the two brothers, Trevar, asked, speaking of the circle of smaller crystal structures not far from this one. "Are they also infused with a god?"

"The gods within our homes are dormant," I said. "Will they come alive once more? We cannot say."

Trevar nodded, his blue eyes wide.

"They abandoned us," Muzzire snarled. "If we die, it's because of them."

"Not so. Although, until only a few years ago, that's what we all believed." Jessia smiled to see us staring at her raptly. "Thanks to our traedor and others like him, some have *awoken*."

Trevar's eyes widened even farther, but he said nothing, just gazed at Jessia with his mouth open.

Jessia stroked his silver hair. "After the disease swept across our world, killing so many of us and even most of our gods—"

One of our younger males gasped, though we'd all heard the story before. Jessia had a way of spinning it in a manner that drew us all in.

"Most of our gods perished from the disease as well, leaving behind their exoskeletons like the ones we now call our homes. Remember, though, your mighty ancestors lived and died here in the Indigan Clan. But our wise leader, Aizor, went with the other clan leaders to speak with the remaining gods in the valley."

To beg, that's what we did. We *begged* the gods to help us. And they told us they would. That was in the spring three years ago, and as the seasons passed, one after another, I'd begun to lose hope that they'd fulfill their promise.

"Soon, the gods said." Jessia's rheumy gaze met mine, and she nodded. "Soon they will send us a sign. They promised to gift us with a future. And when that future is here, our clan will flourish once more."

"'We'll gift you with mates,'" the gods said. "'When we release one to each of you, we'll send a sign that she's your crystal-given bride.'" I nodded at the smiles greeting my words. While the gods didn't indicate who would receive a mate, I prayed I would be among those chosen.

"Many females. That's what the gods promised." Jessia's grin widened, revealing her even white teeth and tusks. "Once they're here, our clans will grow, and we'll be a strong people once more."

Trevar tipped his head back, taking in the crystal structure surrounding us and arching overhead. Moonlight shone through the god's exoskeleton, igniting beams of every variety of blue, making them dance across the floor. A gust of wind swept through the open doorway, stirring the fire, making the shadows shimmer across the blue.

"What sign will our god send?" Trevar's older brother by two years, Brulon, asked.

I shook my head. "We don't know."

"Then it could've happened already," he said with a frown. "And we missed it."

"We should not be doing this," Krute said softly beside me. "They won't be clan. They won't be Zuldruxians."

We'd gone through this many times. "What would you have us do? There are no more mates for us here. They must come from the stars like our gods."

"I don't know." His hard gaze met mine. "But it's not *this*." With that, he rose and stomped from the central crystal structure and out into the night.

I sighed. I was the traedor, not him, though he'd fought me for the honor. That was six years ago. I thought by now he'd accepted the will of the gods and trusted me to make the right decisions for our clan. I'd remind him tomorrow that while I accepted input from everyone, my decision in this was final.

Staring into the fire, I let my distress about Krute pass. This was a time of joy for all the clan, not one of sorrow.

Would I receive the sign soon? If so, then *she'd* join me. She'd love me as much as I did her, and I'd plant many young in her welcoming body.

Jessia stood. "It's time for me to rest." She rubbed her lower back. "My bones are tired. *I'm* tired. But not so tired that I'm ready to leave you all yet. I want to see our clan rejuvenated once more. I feel that time is coming."

Someone gasped, and my gaze was caught by the glow outside.

We all rushed out, staring around, but we couldn't find the source of the light.

Tepesta pointed upward, and we all crooked our heads back.

A crystal shard detached from the main structure and speared down. Something like this had never happened before. It landed in the soil between my feet. Holding my breath, I blinked down at it.

Light blazed from within the shard, and a sudden burn flashed across my right inner forearm. I rolled my hand over to expose my arm in the light, and Muzzire sucked in his breath.

A symbol—that of the Indigan Clan—was etched across my skin in every shade of blue.

At that moment, I *knew*.

At that moment, I felt incredible joy.

Because my mate would arrive shortly.

CHAPTER 3
VANESSA

"It's nearly time," a lilting voice said by my ear, and I woke.

I opened my eyes and blinked up at the plate of glass so close to my nose my exhalations coated it with steam, wondering where I was and what had happened to me.

Memories rushed in of the robocops grabbing me, injecting me with something that made me pass out. Vague memories followed that, of them loading me in a vehicle and driving forever, of one of them slinging me over their shoulder and running, leaping over a very tall fence topped with electrified wire. Sirens rang out, lights flashed, but the robocop carrying me kept going. He didn't stop until he approached . . . I frowned.

The spaceship I'd seen on TV—the one heading to Mars?

Nah, that couldn't be right. No one was allowed close to the launchpad unless they were part of the team.

There was no way the robocop had . . . I remembered

it carrying me inside something that looked an awful lot like the ship before laying me gently inside a long glass cylinder.

One like the arched glass structure encasing me right now.

"Wake," the melodic voice said in a less soothing voice. "Your new life is about to begin."

Whatever I lay in jostled, and with a hum, the glass overhead slid to the right. Mechanical arms lifted me out of the . . . Yes, when I looked down, I could see it was a pod like the ones the people were supposed to sleep in while the ship took them to Mars.

This . . . I couldn't be one of them. I couldn't be on my way to Mars.

The arms drifted across a long room, carrying me above more pods, each containing a woman dressed in a simple white gown that came to their mid-thigh just like the one I now wore. Where had my top gone? My jeans? The apron I'd worn when I worked in the diner's kitchen?

The women inside the pods were stirring, too, and other metal limbs were lifting them, carrying them in a long row behind me.

"Ahhh!" A woman with long red hair cried out. She struggled inside her pod, but the arms only tightened their grip on her arms and lifted her into the air.

I wanted to kick and flail, but I couldn't make my arms and legs do more than flop.

The mechanical arms flew me out of the pod chamber and down a hall with yellow lights flashing on both sides.

Behind me, the other women were woken as well.

"Fuckin' A," someone shouted. "What's going on?"

Another one whimpered.

Others bellowed, and I heard what sounded like an arm or a leg smacking against the wall.

"Talia? Talia!"

"What's happening, Maggie?" The latter voice quavered, and I made my head move, peering back to see two women with long black hair, one with a braid coiled on top of her head, straining their arms out to reach for each other. They had the same facial bone structure and deep brown eyes. Sisters?

The redhead glared at the arms and thrashed her legs.

A woman at the end of the line with curly blonde hair remained slumped in the mechanical arms' grip, her head lolling.

Wake up, I wanted to shout, but I couldn't make my mouth form the words.*Something horrible is happening to us and you need to see.*

"Maggie . . ." Talia cried, big fat tears etching down her face. "I'm scared."

"It's going to be okay. I promise."

Did she truly think she could keep a vow like that? I had no clue what was happening, but whatever it was, it was *bad*, and we had absolutely no control.

The mechanical arms jerked me around a corner, and I noted a track overhead. They appeared to be carrying us through a spaceship, but this couldn't be real. I must be dreaming. I'd finished my shift, gone home, had a nice glass of wine, and I was asleep on the sofa—the usual for me lately.

The track split at the end of a hall, and each of us was channeled into our own path that ended at a door that swept open before we reached it. Inside, I was deposited inside another cylinder. The arms retracted, and a glass lid slid into place above me. Before I could yelp or try to break free, the wall by my feet exploded outward, revealing an endless night scattered with stars and constellations different than any I'd seen before.

The cylinder plunged down a chute like I was part of a bobsled ride to hell, shooting me out into the darkness. On either side of me, other cylinders like mine, each holding a panic-stricken woman, burst from the silver ship. They flew swiftly in a line behind me toward a planet made up of blue, purple, and splatters of red. I'd taken astronomy as an elective, but nothing in the textbook I'd pored through each night gave me a clue of where I could be.

Terror shot through me. Why couldn't I move? What was happening to me?

Where am I?

Lights flashed as the tube holding me plunged through the planet's outer atmosphere and shot toward the surface. A jerk of my head, the only part of me I could move, showed the other cylinders coasting behind and beside mine.

It was night here, and the stars and two slivery moons—two!—shone down on the planet's surface.

I *was* dreaming. None of this could be happening. No,

it wasn't a dream but a nightmare. My scream echoed around me, and breaking free from whatever had restrained me, I clawed at the glass surface overhead, trying to scrape a way through.

Before the pod could smack into the ground, it leveled off, skimming along twenty feet or so about the surface. The other pods holding women split away from mine, heading en masse in another direction. All except one. That one soared somewhere else.

Mountains loomed ahead, and my cylinder flew up over strange, spiky purple trees and dipped down into small valleys covered with tall, stiff golden grasses that barely shifted from the air this pod must be creating.

Its speed slowed as it coasted above stubby trees speckling the slope of a tall mountain. With a screeching whir, it bumped down onto the ground, taking out a few trees that shattered like glass as the pod skimmed along before coming to a jarring stop.

My body kept going, scrunching me into the bottom of the pod.

I screamed again; my voice too shrill for my ears.

The whirring sound ended. Silence echoed with only my ragged breathing and the heavy thud of my heart sounding in my ears.

A hiss rang out, and the top of the pod slid back. Cool air rushed in, making me shiver in the skimpy gown.

At least my body worked. I sat up, clutching the sides and took in a mountain range coated with trees in varying shades of purple. The peaks were golden, a gold similar to what covered the ground around me.

Low thuds grew in volume until they made the cylinder shake. I'd seen enough movies to know that when a person found themselves in a strange world and the ground shook with heavy footsteps, it was a good idea for the main character—who I worried was me—to hide.

A clear open-top pod wasn't going to do a damn thing to protect me.

I scrambled to my knees and bailed over the side of the cylinder, landing hard enough on the rocky soil to knock the wind from my lungs.

More heavy thumps made the ground shake beneath me.

Shit, shit, shit. *Get up, Vanessa!*

I rose to my feet, clinging to the side of the pod, and peered into the dark world surrounding me.

This . . .

. . . wasn't Earth.

Memories of the robocops flashed through my mind. They'd taken me to . . . the freakin' space station and onto the ship destined for Mars. But this wasn't Mars. I'd seen enough footage on TV to know that planet was red, not gold and purple.

Had they stolen the ship?

They must've.

So . . . So . . . Had I been abducted and sent somewhere else?

"No, Vanessa," I whispered. "This is a dream. Any minute now, you're going to wake up and laugh about this. You can tell Franklin all about it during your next shift at the diner."

Heavy footsteps echoed around me. Something big and alien was approaching. I pressed myself against the side of the pod.

I enjoyed sci-fi romance as much as the next woman. Big peens? Take me to your leader. But whatever the enormous thing stomping toward me was, it would have a peen too big for my body to handle. Dino porn was fun and all that when you read it for the titillation factor, but I wasn't ready to start being the vessel for dino young.

Dream or not, it was time to get out of here.

I tiptoed away from the pod, cursing the stupid gown I now wore and . . . what the hell was I wearing on my feet—slippers?

If this was real (ha, it couldn't be!), I was going to complain to the robocop abduction crew for not dressing me appropriately for an outer space adventure. Like, I needed thick canvas clothing, boots, a helmet with a breathing apparatus in case the air I was sucking in much too fast contained microbes that might kill me.

And the pod needed beautification. A cushion might be nice, folks.

A cave along the side of the mountain caught my eye, and I hurried in that direction. For all I knew, the cave might contain something important. Like food and water. A big boulder to hide behind.

Dino condoms.

The stomps grew louder and more furious, and when they were followed by a roar, I spun around.

It wasn't a dino, but it might as well be.

A ten-foot-tall furry beast that reminded me of the abominable snowman only with purple fur scrambled toward me on all fours, sending stubby, darker purple trees flying and leaving literal tracks in the soft soil. His gaze locked on me, and he tipped his head back, beat his chest with his fists, and roared.

"I don't want to stay in this nightmare any longer," I cried shrilly. "Wake up, Vanessa. Wake the ever-loving, fuck up!"

It wasn't working.

Spinning, I raced for the cave, hoping the big opening was too small for Mr. Abominable. Or that it narrowed inside, and I could wedge myself into a crevasse where he couldn't reach.

At least he wasn't sporting a woody—so far.

Something bellowed from my left. Was Mrs. Abominable slamming her way in this direction with a cast iron frying pan in her hand, ready to smack the Mister for playing with his food?

I wasn't going to wait to find out.

I slipped inside the cave, praying this nightmare didn't contain spiders. Or snakes. Or scurrying creatures in general.

While the beast outside continued galloping in my direction, whoever had bellowed came closer as well, still crying out as if he—or she—was about to challenge the world and come up the victor.

The cave was much too shallow and empty of boulders. What kind of nightmare gave me a crappy cave with no place to hide? If I was eaten, the nightmare would be over. Surely, whoever directed things like this wanted to milk out every bit of satisfaction from my sweat.

"Wake up," I hissed to myself, but my mind wasn't listening. It seemed to like this alien world and the beasts stomping closer.

Another cry rang out, hoarse and guttural. As he was ducking down to scramble into the cave along with me, the beast paused.

Teeth chattering, I looked around for a convenient stepping stool. My bones were going to be plucked. I was going to be stewed for dinner—which I guessed was better than becoming his side piece.

In a blur, a second being barreled into the abominable, engaging him in mortal combat with what looked like a long crystal sword. Make that two swords, one held in each of his enormous fists. They slashed through the air like he was a mythical warrior come to life—dressed in only a loincloth. He had tons of muscles, though I really wasn't caring about that right now.

Not too much. Hey, I was a hot-blooded woman. I'd have to lose my sight to miss something like that.

Since I couldn't run, all I could do was press myself against the damp stone wall and watch the scene unfolding in front of the cave.

The abominable swiped out with his big, meaty claws, and the alien male ducked, gouging forward the beast with his crystal blades. One nicked the monster in the shin, and the creature tipped back his head, bellowing in pain. He didn't waste time but stomped toward the crystal-bearing dude with both paws lashing the air.

With a grunt, the alien dove to the side and rolled, coming up in a crouch. He raced toward the monster, flipping up into the air before reaching it, landing on the creature's thigh. He scaled the monster from there, scrambling up the furry chest to the beast's shoulder, where he clung to its head while the abominable thrashed, trying to dislodge him.

One gouge with a crystal blade, and the furry creature staggered. He swayed and plunged toward the cave, landing face down with a heavy thud, blocking the lower half of the opening.

The alien peeled himself off and stood by the monster's back, panting, before sheathing his blades in a belt on his waist and turning toward me. His glowing teal eyes penetrated the gloom, locking on me cringing against the back wall.

With a grunt, he swaggered toward me as if I was the spoils of war and it was time to do some plundering.

Yelping, I looked around for a way to escape, spying a hole above me, though it appeared too high to jump and grab onto the edge. But I could scale the wall. People did stuff like that all the time. Not me, but there was a first time for everything. I stuffed my right slipper into a small crevasse and stepped up, sliding the tips of my fingers into a crack. My left foot was easily wedged into another fissure, but when I reached up with my left hand to poke my fingers into a hole in the wall, the alien reached me.

He huffed and wrapped a big brawny arm that had to be the size of a leg around my waist. He hauled me off the wall and tossed me over his shoulder.

"Wait. No," I cried, flailing.

He growled a string of guttural grunts punctuated with what sounded like barks, his big palm coming down on my ass.

"Hey, don't!" I squirmed, smacking his rippling, muscular back with my fists. "Let me go. Please."

My voice echoed in the cave as he strode out into the night, the steady pad of his footsteps taking me around the abominable and down the hillside.

The crystal structures I'd seen as the pod coasted above the surface winked below, every color of blue imaginable oozing in rippling waves as if they'd trapped their own version of the northern lights and were in a competition to see who could outshine the rest.

He paused at the top of the hill and released a low call that sounded like "Awww-whoop-whoop-whoop!"

Thunder erupted, and I peered up at the sky, expecting a deluge to add to my kidnapping-by-alien nightmare, but the sky remained clear.

Something moved to our right, the trees swaying as whatever it was rushed through the forest.

Did the abominable have friends?

A creature resembling a crystal triceratops burst from the trees and stomped toward us, its scales glistening deep blue in the moonlight.

It shook its head, the thin, clear blue flaps like enormous ears on either side of its head flopping.

Lowering its head, it bellowed and charged toward us, the long glassy spears jutting from the sides of its jaw thrashing through the air.

Fuck, it was going to kill us.

CHAPTER 4

AIZOR

"None of that, now, Voolon," I said firmly as my beast frolicked over to us, playfully flapping her exoears. She shook her head and butted me with her snout before sniffing the female who scrambled around in my arms, muttering words I couldn't understand. "This is serious," I chided my mount. "I hold my mate, my true one, the female who'll soon gift me with many young."

Voolon huffed and settled. She was a well-behaved beast, and I was grateful to have her. I'd raised her since she hatched from an egg, feeding her juicy bites of meat and grooming her scaled hide as often as I could. She rewarded my care by allowing me to ride on her back.

"This is Voolon," I told my mate. At least she'd stopped wiggling around, though she was so tiny, I could easily restrain her if need be. Easing her forward and into the cradle of my arms, I frowned down at her while she looked up at me with what I hoped was excitement. I worried terror shone in her oddly green eyes. I'd never seen eyes in that color, and they stunned me for a heartbeat. Then I reminded myself we weren't secure here. I needed to get her to safety before I allowed myself to fully examine her face, hair, and body. "I'm Aizor, traedor of the Indigan Clan, which is the best of them all, though you'll soon see this."

She blinked up at me. I juggled her a bit to hold her with one arm and pointed to my chest.

"Aizor," I said slowly, repeating it a few more times.

My mate made a few gulping sounds, sucking in air each time.

Pray that the fates hadn't sent me a mate who was deficient. I'd cherish her regardless, but it would be nice to have someone to talk to, to stand by my side.

I leaped up onto Voolon's back and settled my mate on my lap, facing me, placing her legs around my body and her arms around my torso—though her arms were much too short to reach, and she only clung to my sides limply.

Her hair, secured in a long weave along her spine, flopped around. So strange that she didn't wear it loose like a Zuldruxian female. It was also an odd color, that of the soil deep found on the floor within some of our caves, yet with strands that rivaled the golden towers of our central crystal god structure.

She kept muttering and flailing, releasing the same *waaaa* sound. Was my mate alright? I worried my tusks, hoping it was so.

What were the gods thinking of when they matched me with such a peculiar creature?

No matter. If she behaved and spoke like an adult, we'd make this work.

While my mate clung to my torso as she should, appearing to gape down at Voolon before looking up at me with an equally stunned expression, I urged my mount to turn. Voolon start down the hillside, loping toward the valley. I rocked with her lolling gait, shifting my hips to accommodate the motion.

"Waaaa!" my mate said.

"Waaaa," I agreed, though not as loudly as her. I'd just defeated one predator. There was no need to call the attention of another. It was too bad the beast's meat tasted rank. There was enough there to feed a clan for many seasons. In the morning, I'd send some males to cut away the biggest sections to feed our hepadons. They often grazed but they adored fleshy treats.

My mate muttered something against my chest. It appeared the gods had gifted me with a female who couldn't speak my language. We'd find a way to communicate once I had her inside our home and on my bed furs.

She must know she was mine. That would be expected from a true mate. She must also know we'd soon be rutting.

Eager to reach the pen where we kept our hepadons during the night and where food awaited her, Voolon broke into a gallop, flinging herself down the hillside. The heavy thud of her hooves echoed around us, making small creatures in the low brush along the side of the trail scatter.

My mate made more odd sounds that must be her way of expressing her eagerness to become my bride.

"Are you hungry for me, my precious one?" I asked, gently using a finger to lift her chin. Her skin was incredibly soft and pale when compared to my blue. Another oddity I'd get used to.

"Waaaa," she cried out again.

Showing her my tusks in a grin, a gesture sure to impress her, I made the waaaa sound as well, wondering what it meant. Hepadons had no language outside of grunts only they appeared to understand. My mate could come from a species like that. If so, I'd have to study her sounds to see if I could sense a difference. I wanted to learn how to communicate with her.

How else would I know how to please her in bed?

CHAPTER 5
VANESSA

S till a dream. Still a dream. Still a dream!

No matter how many times I repeated the phrase in my mind, I wasn't convincing myself it was true.

Surely, I was back home in my bed, sleeping. I'd wake in the morning, shake my head about my vivid imagination, and get ready for another shift at the diner.

The creature galloping beneath me felt much too real.

So did the cock rising under the loincloth of the male alien who held me. Fuck, I was going to be raped in my dream. Whose mind made up shit like that?

As if he was worried I'd fall, he tightened his arms around me and rested his chin on the top of my head. He was warm and he smelled amazing, like leather and a spice I was unfamiliar with but would crave for the rest of my life. This would fit with a dream. I'd always had a thing for sci-fi romance, let alone blue alien guys, the ice ones. That must be why my mind had taken me in this direction while I was asleep.

Talk about a fantasy feeling incredibly real, though.

The rocking motion smoothed me, and I bit back a yawn. My eyelids drooped, but I snapped them open once more, taking in the scruffy dark purple trees growing along the wide path where the crystal beast galloped.

After suppressing another yawn, I couldn't keep my eyes open any longer. I dropped into sleep within my sleep . . .

In my next dream, someone carried me with so much gentleness it made my heart ache. They stopped walking, saying something in a guttural voice, and chatter erupted around us in the same language. Someone touched my arm and their voice got louder.

I couldn't make myself wake up.

When the person holding me started walking again, I slipped into another lovely dream where the yummy smelling alien male laid me on a bed of furs. Now this was a true fantasy of mine. Normally, I'd be appalled by the thought of lying on dead animal skins. In a dream? Why not?

I was jostled back and forth, and my arms tugged in a couple of directions before I was covered with yet another fur. I snuggled down into the softness, breathing in the light scent of fresh air and flowers, and luxuriated in how amazing the furs felt against my bare skin.

In reality, I'd be horrified to think fuzzy animals had died to create my bedding, but this was a dream. Might as well savor the rich feeling, knowing I'd wake up to simple blankets.

A cool draft of air sliced down my spine, but even that couldn't drag me out of the wonder I floated in.

Until a warm body snuggled into my back and pressed his cocks against my ass.

His hand landed on my breast, and he rolled the nipple.

I shrieked and sat up, staring down at the alien from my dream—*nightmare!*

Scrambling away from him, I burst from the big bed, staggering across a smooth surface. I grabbed the first thing I found to cover my naked body—a strip of leather lying on the floor. It wasn't wide enough to cover my breasts unless I scrunched them together.

Something scraped and a light bloomed.

I got my first, second, no, make that third look at . . . my bedmate.

Heaven help me, but this wasn't a dream.

Realizing what I clutched against my front, I held it away from my body, grimacing. "This is your loincloth."

"It is," he said softly, one side of his thick brow ridge lifting in a sardonic manner. His impossibly Caribbean-blue eyes gleamed with humor, which riled me up even more.

"Dirty or clean?" I bit out.

He shrugged. "Why should I care?"

Shit, I was trapped in a . . . I peered around. Trapped in a round two-story blue crystal structure topped with white that appeared about twenty feet across. A crystal yurt, that's what it was.

Anyway. I was trapped inside this odd place with a big, too-appealing alien guy who, like every other man I'd met, tossed his clothes on the floor whether they were clean or dirty. As if the cleaning lady—who would not be me—would come by, scoop them up, and "magically" return them to his bureau as clean as they were before he wore them.

No bureau in sight.

Since his dubious loincloth was all I had to cover myself with, I stretched it across the front of my body.

"Leave me alone," I snarled.

He sat up, giving me a look of confusion. "But you're my crystal-given mate." He gestured to the luxurious furs he lay on. "Come back to bed, my pretty one, and I'll plant our first youngling in your belly."

A feeling I couldn't define coiled around my spine. Whatever it was sent warm tendrils to my core. As if I wanted to have a kid with this guy? Never.

"You're not a dream." I shook my head, hoping that would clear my mind. "I should be in my apartment, kicking myself out of bed and straggling into the kitchen to eat something appropriate for breakfast. Like tacos."

His head cocked, and I couldn't miss the way something else was *cocked* to lift the furs below his belly.

"You fiend," I shrieked.

Wait a second right there.

"I understand what you're saying," I whispered. "No more guttural gobbledygook. And you understand me."

"And here I thought you were sick or something."

"What does that have to do with anything?"

"You kept wailing and thrashing, no matter what I said. Can you blame me for thinking there might be something wrong with you?"

"You were going to stuff you cock inside someone who might be sick?"

He winced. "Only with your permission, of course."

"Well, I haven't granted it." I shrugged off the direction the conversation was heading. "Where am I?"

"In our home, my pretty one." He smiled, his lips curling deliciously around his tusks.

"I'm not your pretty anything."

"What else can I call you? You haven't told me your name. I'm Aizor, traedor of the Indigan Zuldrux Clan. I introduced myself after I killed the abadeer in the cave, though you didn't understand. You may call me Aizor. No title needed."

"I'm Vanessa Smith, exclusive chef of Dria's Diner, a fine dining establishment back on Earth. You can call me Vanessa, no title needed either."

"Van-eesa."

Close enough.

"Zuldrux. Is that your species?"

He pressed his fist against his chest. "The Zuldrux have lived in this area since longer than anyone can remember."

Species, then.

"The crystal gods sent you to me, Van-eesa," he said. "I saw you arrive from the sky. You should've waited for me to come for you instead of attracting the abadeer's attention."

"Crystal gods?" This was something straight out of a bizarre sci-fi movie.

"Our clan traedors beseeched the gods to give us mates." He held out his arm, twisting it to show off the underside. "See? The gods told me you, my mate, would be with me soon, and I'd be given a sign to show me you were mine. This is the sign."

I tiptoed forward, though I stayed beyond the reach of his muscular arms, and studied the marking on his forearm. "It's a tattoo. Everyone has them. Not me, not yet. It means nothing."

"A tat . . ." His smile only deepened. "It's a sign from our crystal god."

"You're out of your mind."

He frowned. "My mind is very much . . . within me still."

I was beginning to believe this could be real. The robocops kidnapped me, placed me on the ship to Mars that somehow deviated to bring me here instead. Did that mean the other women I'd seen in pods were on this planet too?

"Besides, you have one too," he said, pointing to my arm. "It's god given, just like me."

What was he . . .? I gaped down at my arm. "Where did this come from?" I shrieked, rubbing at the tattoo that eerily matched his. It was pretty if I was into couple's tattoos—but I wasn't. "Take it off."

"The gods gave it to you to prove you're mine," he drawled. "Now do you believe?"

I stomped my foot, making my boobs jiggle. "No!"

Spying my skimpy abduction pod nightie lying on the floor, I crowed and scooped it up, waving it around in the air before pivoting to face away from him. After flipping the loincloth over my back to somewhat cover my ass from his view, I wrangled into the gown, trying not to moon him.

After ditching the loincloth, I turned, feeling slightly better now that I was clothed, though still disconcerted about the "mating" tattoos. Mine would come off with water. Or a good scrubbing. Then I could tell him we'd obtained a crystal divorce.

"You appear upset," he said, his sultry gaze dancing down my frame, practically undressing me all over again. I could *feel* his gaze like he was touching me.

And that only irritated me. "I'm pissed off. Those damn robocops. They . . ." I tilted my head. "You didn't bring me here."

"Our crystal god did." His voice had taken on a smooth seductiveness that nearly lulled me. "Come to bed. We'll celebrate our mating, and I'll happily plant our first youngling in your belly."

"It doesn't grow in a belly but a uterus, you . . . you . . . alien." The word didn't sound like much of an insult.

"I'm a Zuldrux warrior. *Your* Zuldrux warrior. I'll cherish you. Kiss the very feet you walk on. Love you for a lifetime."

"What about massage?" I quipped, only joking.

"I'll happily rub all of you from your feet to the top of your head."

Some guys offered flowers. This one seemed to think he'd impress me with a foot massage—which he might.

He grunted, and his smile replaced the scowl, both of which made him highly attractive.

He was a complete rogue, and I'd always been partial to bad boys. They were my downfall back on Earth, which was why I'd ended up working at a diner. My ex was one bad boy too many, and I was now on a bad boy hiatus.

"Back up a sec. Did you say you *love* me?" How could this be real?

"I will. The gods sent you to me, which means you're my perfect match."

"Look, you can't just run around making promises like that. I could have bad breath in the morning. Bedhead. Stinky feet you won't want to kiss, let alone massage. For all you know, I'm cranky until I've had three cups of coffee." I was. Totally was. "You might hate me once you get to know me."

He shrugged. "The gods wouldn't gift you to me unless they knew I'd love you." He waved to his cock still poking away at the lush furry bedding. "Join me on our bed, mate. You will soon love *me*. Cherish me. Kiss the very feet I walk on."

"I don't do feet. And you can't just . . . assume we're going to love each other because of that." I pointed to his tattoo.

As much as I wanted to tell myself none of this was

real, that it was all a dream, I knew in my heart I was wide awake.

I didn't believe in crystal gods or any of the stuff he was spouting, but I knew one thing.

Crystal beings had sent robocops to kidnap me and bring me here to be gifted to this big brawny alien.

CHAPTER 6
AIZOR

My mate wasn't convinced we were meant to be together. How could I show her she was the light of my very existence, the only one I'd cherish forever? I wasn't a harsh male. Most would call me kind. Gentle, even, on occasion.

And infinitely patient.

I'd give her time to get used to the idea and *then* I'd plant my first youngling within her glorious body.

I wasn't sure why I could understand her now when I hadn't been able to before, but I accepted the intervention of our gods. They'd brought her to me, and now they'd given us the gift of communication. I would give thanks the next time I visited the island's crystal structure.

"Come lie down," I said softly, patting the bed furs. I didn't wish to frighten my pretty new mate. "This will make more sense in the morning." If she bolted from our home, I'd chase her and bring her back, of course, but I'd prefer for her to remain here because she understood that this was where she belonged.

"I'm not sleeping with you," she snarled.

"Where else will you rest?"

"Somewhere. I don't know." She looked so dejected my heart twisted into a knot. I pushed back the furs and stood.

Gulping, she stared at my erect cock. "Shit, it's as blue as the rest of you."

"Why would it be any other color?"

"And you have two of them!"

"I'd be a defective male if I didn't." I looked down, and because she appeared shocked, I almost expected to find something peculiar between my legs.

"What . . . What does the second, smaller one do?" She nibbled on her long blue claws.

"It enjoys sucking on clits."

"Shit, don't say things like that."

I shrugged.

"Stop trying to seduce me," she snapped.

"When I try to seduce you, my pretty mate, you'll know it," I purred.

"Fuck that and the spaceship it rode in on. Where am I, anyway?"

"I've brought you to my home." I tapped the wall. "Each of us lives within a dead god, and it protects us."

The fluffy strips above her eyes lifted. "Dead god?"

"They died long ago, though a few still survive."

"Okay. I guess understanding that part has a steep learning curve." She shook her head. She'd done it so often I was beginning to wonder if the gesture was some sort of tic. If so, I'd ask the healer to see her. Perhaps there was a cure.

"I assume we understand each other because the gods have chosen to intervene. You belong to me, you're my mate, and they want you to understand the world around you."

"This is real, isn't it?" she wailed, yanking on her glorious hair. "I'm not dreaming."

"No."

"I've been abducted by robocops along with a bunch of other women, and we've been deposited on an uncharted planet far from Earth."

I didn't understand much of what she said, but I could piece together what she might mean. As for the other women, I wasn't the only male who'd begged for a mate.

"Crystal gods don't exist." She said it with such certainty that even I'd believe her if she wasn't standing in front of me, evidence of their intervention.

She would soon see.

"You don't happen to have a handy spaceship to take me back to Earth, do you?"

"I don't know what a spaceship is. I ride my voolon from one destination to another, but I don't believe she'll be able to take you to this Earth since we don't know where it is." Or what it was.

"Earth is a planet. It's where I come from." She whimpered, and she wrapped her arms around her waist, hugging herself. It made me sad to see her do this rather than take comfort from me. Would a day come when my mate would seek me for love and affection?

I had to hope the gods hadn't been wrong in gifting her to me. There would be no future for me without her, yet I'd never force her to remain with me if she begged to leave for . . . Eard. No, *Earth.*

"I'll do my best to discover where your home is." Couldn't she see that her home was with me? My heart felt heavy. It was hard to form words, and I sensed the right ones would be vital now. I couldn't risk driving her away. "Will you remain with me until I consult the gods?"

"I suppose I can do that."

I grabbed a clean loincloth and wrapped it around my waist, hiding my cocks from her view. If she didn't want me, showing her that I had the necessary tools to please her wouldn't make a difference.

She was here with me, for now.

But stark loneliness filled me.

I'd do anything—*give* anything—not to lose her.

CHAPTER 7
VANESSA

"You may sleep on our—*the*—bed tonight," he said.

"Where will you sleep?" I stifled a yawn. I'd been through the wringer, and I'd only been here a short time. I could only imagine what a week or a month would be like in this strange, primitive world.

"I'll gather more furs and lie nearby."

"There's no Super 8 in the vicinity?" At his frown, I sighed. "Never mind. You can share the crystal yurt with me. No harm in that as long as you promise not to get touchy feely when I'm out. I'll smack you, and I've got a mean fist. You don't want to test me."

He grinned and lifted my hand. "This tiny thing? It would do no more harm than the nibble of a fless."

I tugged my hand away. "Yeah, well, don't push it."

He nodded slowly, and I was grateful he didn't appear to be one of those alpha dudes who'd force this. "Tomorrow, we'll travel to the clan meeting grounds where we'll speak with the gods and find a way to help you."

"I appreciate that."

He grunted. I could tell he wasn't pleased. How could he be? He believed I was his god-chosen mate, which, when you thought about it, might give a girl a bit of a thrill if she was into junk like that.

I wasn't.

But still.

He thought I was sent here to love him forever, and he seemed sad that I didn't already.

"Love takes time," I said.

"Yes."

His voice sounded hollow, his anguish biting into me, making a searing pain spread through my chest. I didn't like it one bit.

"I don't suppose you have a toothbrush and paste?" I asked. "I have a feeling I haven't brushed in . . . light years." My shrill laugh rang out. It was either laugh or burst into tears. If I did that, I suspected I'd never stop.

I needed sleep. Coffee in the morning along with a plate full of burritos with extra guac. A long soak in a tub with oodles of rose-scented bubbles.

All of which I had a feeling I'd never see again in my life.

"No brush, but if you mean for your . . ." His gaze fell on my mouth. "You have no tusks."

"Good observation." The words popped out, though kindly. I flashed my pearly whites that were only straight due to good genetics. Thanks, parents, for that at least.

"We use this to keep our tusks clean." He crossed the room and grabbed a handwoven basket full of items.

Handwoven. Everything here was handmade. Nothing would come from a machine. No computers. No cell phones. No electricity.

The only saving grace was that there would be no robocops either.

He pulled out a stick about the length of my forearm. One end bristled with short things that vaguely looked like the strands on a feather. I touched them, finding them soft yet stiff. "We use this and this." He presented me with the stick and a small, covered pottery bowl holding a purple goo that, when I sniffed it, smelled vaguely like flowers, though it had a sharp tang that tingled in my sinuses.

"Do you have water?"

He lifted a flask, flashing his tusks. Really, he was kind of cute when he did that, so I wished he wouldn't. I might be here for some time, and the last thing I needed was to become attached to a male who thought he was my husband.

A tingle shot down my spine and zoomed over to tease my clit. I ignored it.

"I'll, um, brush and spit outside, I guess." I waved to the leather flap draped across the only opening in the crystal structure.

He followed me outside, where I brushed my teeth and rinsed, spitting around the side of the blue glassy building. I also took a long swallow of the water, then some more, because it tasted amazing. No metallic flavor and not a hint of plastic or bleach.

Score one for the aliens.

Pleased enough with the results, I peered around, taking in the big blue crystal yurts similar to Aizor's and set up in a big ring.

"These must be other homes for your . . . clan members."

He frowned, and his gaze locked on an area above us.

Turning, I peered in that direction, seeing subtle movement. Was someone up there, nearly hidden among the trees? Fear spiked through me. I knew nothing about this world or these people.

Or what might be watching from the woods.

Aizor grunted and a male on the other side of the open area shifted away from the side of a blue crystal building. His sharp gaze slid down my frame and more chills ripped through me. I didn't know this male, but he didn't seem happy to see me.

When Aizor snarled and tucked me behind his bulky frame, the other guy lifted his arm. Two more males rushed over to stand with him, hefting swords like the ones Aizor had used to kill the abominable beast after I arrived.

The three males melted behind the crystal buildings.

Aizor continued to stare toward where I thought I'd seen someone—though there didn't appear to be anyone there any longer.

Not long later, I spied the three males flitting through the woods near that location, jogging upward.

"Who was up there?" I asked.

Aizor said nothing, just kept squinting in that direction.

Maybe his . . . guards, or whoever they were, would take care of the problem—assuming there *was* a problem.

My skin still rippled with unease, but I felt relatively safe with Aizor and his alien army nearby.

The moons generated a lot of light, like half of what we got back on Earth from sunshine, though the light contained a vaguely purple hue.

Turning, I took in the small valley with enormous mountains and cliffs all around. On the other side of the big open area, I could barely make out a splice in the mountains, a pass they could travel through, assuming they did much traveling. And beyond the mountains, something vast glistened. An ocean? The moonlight highlighted a bigger valley to my right, peppered with more crystal structures, though none in blue.

Feeling overwhelmed and incredibly tiny when compared to this vast world, I handed Aizor the flask. "I, um, want to go to bed now." My teeth chattered, but I kept telling myself everything would be alright. I drummed up a smile for Aizor as I tugged aside the leather flap. "Please tell me you don't snore."

He huffed and looked at me so oddly, I paused.

When he spoke, only a bunch of gobbledygook came out.

CHAPTER 8
AIZOR

The gods, in their infinite wisdom, had decided my mate would only understand me if we remained inside our home. Or inside any crystal structure, perhaps. We'd test this in the morning.

She stared at me in shock as I tugged her back inside.

I marveled at how her nonsense words suddenly became understandable the moment we crossed the threshold and the flap swung back into place.

"What just happened?" she asked, tugging away from my grip.

It hurt that my mate didn't want to be close to me, but I reminded myself to be patient as I explained my assumption.

"Let's test it again." She slipped from our home before I could say a word, and I followed.

Everyone else had gone to bed, but it was late. Only the guards had remained awake. I would introduce her to my clan in the morning.

She turned to face me and spoke, her voice lifting in frustration when I shrugged. I replied, and her face tightened further. She stomped back inside our home, and I joined her, securing the flap for the night.

"This . . . is bad news," she said. "How am I going to find my way home if the only person I can talk to is you and only when we're inside this building?" Her hand flicked out to the crystal surrounding us.

"We'll find a way to communicate when we're outside." I wasn't too distressed about it.

"I suppose." With a sigh, she sat on our bed.

I untied and tossed aside my loincloth.

Her widening eyes dropped to my cocks before she slapped her hands against her cheeks. "Um, Aizor. Boundaries?"

"I understand clan boundaries, but I don't believe that's what you're referring to."

"You took off your clothing."

"Don't you remove yours when you sleep?"

"Where I come from, being naked with a guy in bed is taken as an invitation."

I huffed. "I've told you I won't rut with you tonight. You can trust my word."

"I just met you, so how can I do something like that? And don't think I haven't noticed that you only said *tonight*, not for the rest of my life."

"I'll never promise anything like that."

"I'm still wearing this nightie to bed."

"And tomorrow? Will you wear it all day as well?"

"Why not?"

"I suppose you could. The gods might be offended." They *would* be offended, but perhaps they could be as patient as me.

"Well, welcome to my world. I'm offended with them right now too."

"If you want them to help you, you need to worship them as we do," I said.

"It doesn't work that way. And I'm still wearing this."

"We'll go to the pools, and you can wash it."

"There's no laundromat here, I suppose?"

"I don't believe so."

"Other than the crystal thing you've got going, you appear to live like a caveman. Crystal house. Crystal spears—"

"Swords, please." I gestured to them resting on a wooden table, still in their leather sheaths and secured to a belt. I'd removed them earlier and would don them when I left my home in the morning.

Her eyes spiraled in a circle. "Okay, swords, then. You wear a leather loincloth. You battled a beast outside a cave."

I smiled at where she was taking our conversation. "As you pointed out, we don't *live* in caves."

"Semantics."

My mate used such odd words. They made sense, yet they didn't.

Opening the trunk I'd crafted from wood with my own hands, I tugged out my bundle of spare furs. I untied them and spread them out on the floor beside my usual bed.

Someone scratched on the door, and I secured my loincloth around my waist again before letting them inside.

"Krute," I said. "What did you find?" He'd returned after searching the area for intruders.

"I saw one of Nevarn's males up in the hills."

"They dare to come this close?"

"He's much too bold. We should attack his clan to remind them that they need to remain within their own territory."

I was hesitant to do this. Not because I wasn't willing to battle. I never shied away from something like that. But starting a clan war?

I glanced at my new mate who I'd do anything to protect.

"We can't stand back and allow them to do this." Krute followed my gaze. His face remained neutral, but he'd been clear that he wasn't any happier about the gods' mate plan than Muzzire.

"I don't intend to."

"What do you want us to do?" His attention returned to me.

"Broaden the guards' reach."

"And if they come across other Celedar Clan males?" A direct challenge came through in his voice.

"We defend our territory," I said grimly. "No matter what that takes."

His grunt showed approval, thankfully. Battling Nevarn and his males was one thing, but fighting with someone within my own clan? I'd avoid that as long as possible.

"Very well." With that, he left.

I grumbled for a moment.

"Bad news?" she asked.

"Nothing I can't handle." I nodded to reinforce that thought within my own mind and tossed aside my loincloth again. "Let's rest."

My mate may state she wasn't interested in me, but her gaze raked down my body. My cocks perked up, hoping for between-the-furs activity, but they would soon settle back down.

Patience, I reminded them.

Dropping onto the pile of furs I'd spread out, I settled on my back.

Van-eesa eased onto my bed, sliding between the furs. Her intent gaze remained on me as if she suspected I'd pounce.

"No groping me during the night," she mumbled, shaking a finger my way. "Stay on your fur pile, and I'll do the same."

Sitting, I extinguished the light, and its pungent smoke perfumed the air. I laid back on the furs, "When I *grope* you, it will not be a rough fumble."

"Every guy under the sun says things like that. They assume women are panting for their touch. Not this girl."

"You'll soon welcome my affection." I spoke with complete certainty, though I did have my doubts.

"Leave it to a guy to come up with a line like that."

My mate was . . . surly. Unwelcoming. And somewhat demanding.

Yet I would still love her. I'd give her my undying devotion for the rest of my life and pray that one day she felt the same.

"Do you know that many times when a guy's humping away on a woman, she's either thinking about what she'll cook for dinner or pretending to be into it?" she asked in the darkness.

I wasn't exactly sure what she meant. "Are you suggesting you won't enjoy my rutting? That you'll be thinking about meat?"

"*Exactly.*"

I chuckled. "Not while my second cock is sucking on your clit."

"You're not in a position to unleash your second cock anywhere near my clit."

I would be.

It was something to strive for. The gods would not have sent her to me if she wouldn't love me or welcome my cocks.

"Let's go to sleep," she said. "Maybe I'll wake up in my own bed and discover this was just a nightmare."

"Sleep well, my pretty mate. Tomorrow, I'll start teaching you about our clan and your duties here."

"Yeah, that's going to be interesting."

"And by the end of the day, you'll tell me you welcome my touch."

CHAPTER 9

VANESSA

Somehow, I slept. I woke at the crack of dawn, when sunlight pierced the top of the crystal structure, making about fifty thousand different variations of blue slash across the bed furs and poke at my eyes.

Groaning, I rubbed my face. I'd hoped this was a nightmare, but instead, I was still stuck on a distant plant.

I was snuggling against a big, muscular alien who'd remained in his own bed while I'd migrated from mine. I'd draped my arm across his beastly chest. I'd hitched my left leg up across the tops of his thighs. And he had a hard-on.

In the sci-fi romance novels I adored, every heroine in a situation like this would yelp and scramble from the bed. She'd flutter her hands at her throat and snarl at the alien, pissed off at him for being turned on just by lying beside her. Well, by her essentially lying on top of him with her leg rubbing his hard-on, that is.

Stop it, I barked at my leg.

The stupid thing reluctantly obeyed, though it remained on top of his big old stiffy.

I eased away from him, planning to sneak outside and see if I could find a bathroom. After that, I'd look for my space pod. If there were controls inside, I'd figure them out. I could hop in, close the hatch, and make it take me back to Earth. In my new fantasy, it would zip up into the sky. In no time, it would land on Earth. The military would descend after spying my pod soaring across the sky, and I'd explain that I was abducted but had found a way home. They'd run scans on my brain and body, declare me mostly sane and healthy, and release me. Then I could return to my job at the diner.

Adios, Aizor the alien. Sayonara, blue crystal world.

Since my nightie barely came to my mid-thigh, I tugged one of the furs off my bed and draped it around me. A quick glance at Aizor showed he was still sleeping.

With a sly grin, I nudged aside the leather door flap and trotted outside.

"Ah," I cried when I slammed into a blue-skinned alien with four boobs walking past the front of Aizor's crystal home.

The woman looked me up and down, her thick unibrow lifting. She was clutching a baby to her chest and dressed in a brown tunic decorated with gold trim that came to her knees and was tucked in at her waist with a sparkly gold belt.

Nearby, other aliens stopped what they were doing

and gaped at me. A few whispered, though even if they shouted, I knew I wouldn't understand what they said.

I only spied a few women—all with four breasts stacked in a square on their chests. Each wore something similar to the woman standing beside me.

Where could I get an outfit like that? At least it would cover my ass and wouldn't be almost see-through like the crystal-bestowed nightie I now wore. And the belt was gorgeous.

The woman released a string of guttural words I couldn't understand.

I winced and did the same, telling her about the last time I'd volunteered at the animal shelter and the cats we still hoped would find forever homes for. I could've been discussing the weather, my dying need for a hot cup of coffee, or my upcoming period. Shit. Period. I doubted this group even knew what a tampon was.

Or double shit, it might be made of crystal. Not shoving anything like that inside my body.

Seeing my look of horror, the woman's frown deepened.

Way to make a good first impression. I drummed up a smile and reeled away from her, slamming into yet another alien.

Aizor wrapped his arms around me and grumbled a string of words by my ear. I could guess what he was saying.

Where did you go, my pretty mate?

Are you sure you don't want to play with my second peen?

Play? Maybe.

Take it for a test run?

Like a flash flood roaring through a culvert, heat pooled between my legs. Why was my mind taking me in a steamy direction?

He spoke to the woman, and she gave me a tentative, tusk-filled smile, still talking away while shifting her arm to show me her baby.

Such a cutie! I cooed and stroked the child's gorgeous blue face. The baby slept, ignoring the human blathering on about her gorgeous, tufted white hair and her tiny little tusks jutting up from her lower jawline.

Baby lust consumed me.

Until I caught Aizor's proprietary eye and remembered his vow to plant younglings inside my belly. Uterus. Whatever.

"Vanessa," I said, tapping my chest.

"Van-eesa."

"Not bad." I grinned at the woman.

She tapped her chest. "Tapesta." And then stroked the baby's head. "Wellire."

"Tapesta," I repeated. "Pretty little Wellire."

Aizor looked around at those gathering nearby, peering our way, and shouted out a long string of words ending in Van-eesa. Everyone nodded and a few gave me bows before returning to whatever they were doing.

With a nod and her own bow, Tapesta strode across the open area and ducked inside a crystal structure on the opposite side of the one I'd slept in.

I pinched the corner of Aizor's loincloth and tugged him back into his home, trying to ignore his glorious blue-skinned, muscular physique. When had I gotten a lady hard-on for this alien beast? Sure, he had a build that suggested he lifted weights 24/7, and there was that second, clit-sucking peen to consider, but I couldn't let my mind head in that direction. I was leaving this place as soon as I could buy a one-way ticket back to Earth.

I'd be foolish to let myself become emotionally involved with him or anyone else in his clan.

"You should've woken me up, my pretty mate," he said, his fingertips teasing across my arm.

Since the gesture made my insides tingle and more fluid gush between my legs, I backed out of his reach. "I have to use the facilities."

He frowned. "What are facilities?"

"I need to pee."

"Pee." His frown wasn't easing. "What is this pee, Van-eesa?"

Yeah, I definitely needed to figure out what I'd use during my period if I remained here much longer. No way would I try to explain that to Aizor.

Squatting, I swept my arm from my back end and outward in a dramatic gesture while making a sound I hoped sounded like flowing water.

His chuckle rang out. "I believe I know what you need."

"I'm sure you do," I said dryly. In more ways than one. At least he couldn't tell how much his simple gestures turned me on.

Thankfully, he didn't tumble me onto the furs to go

exploring between my legs for confirmation. He took my hand and led me out of his home.

Pausing at each alien we passed to introduce me, followed by them bowing—even to me, now—Aizor led me away from the circle of crystal structures, past a huge pen holding glassy-ish purple dinos like the one he'd ridden last night, and over to a row of crystal buildings fused to the side of the hill. No *Ladies* or *Gents* noted on the leather flaps outside two of them, but I understood when he swept one aside and gestured for me to enter.

"Braline," he said.

"Bathroom."

"Braline. Braff-roon."

This was the beginning of us understanding each other outside his home. At this rate, I should be able to tell him what I needed in about twenty years. Still, it was a start, and I appreciated his eagerness to help me even if I wasn't going to be here long enough to learn more words than I had fingers.

Since it was dark inside the *braline*, I paused to let my eyes adjust before moving toward tall wooden structures mounted across the back wall. For a bathroom, it smelled amazing, like fresh air and flowers.

The tall stone structures didn't have steps, and if these were toilets, they'd been crafted for people who were two feet taller than me. I peered into the opening at the top of one of them and gulped to see the hole drop away what looked like forever. Stone covered the sides, and when a gust of wind swept up, hitting my face, it smelled like flowers. Squares of cloth rested on the back.

Nothing beat soft toilet paper. The toilet people back on Earth could learn some new tricks from the Zuldruxians.

I really had to pee, so I peered around, hoping to find a stool or rock I could use to help me climb to the top. Nada. What did little kids do?

With a shrug, I gripped the edge of the structure and launched myself upward, smacking onto my belly across the top. Some scrambling put me in the right position, and after hitching my underwear down, I did my business, using one of the cloths to wipe. Should I toss it into the hole? I couldn't tell if it was biodegradable, but since I didn't see any bucket to throw it away or a place to leave it, I gingerly dropped it down the hole, watching as it was swept away by the flower-scented wind.

Since there were no sinks for washing, I left the building, finding Aizor waiting outside. He nodded as if he could tell my bladder was no longer screaming at me and started back toward the ring of crystal buildings.

I tapped his arm, and when he stopped, I made a rubbing my hands together gesture. "I need to wash."

"Ah. Wevire abreck."

Sure. Maybe.

He led me past the toilet buildings and around a bend on a well-trodden trail. Approaching a regular old cave entrance about two stories high at the top of the opening, he took me inside.

As if there was a sophisticated motion detector system near the entrance, lights bloomed overhead, pale blue crystal blobs that wiggled and generated enough light for me to see smooth, dark purple stone walls and a brownish-yellow dirt floor.

"Lectum," he said, pointing to the blobs.

"Light," I said.

He nodded. Maybe this could be fun. I'd always wanted to learn a new language. Now was my chance.

However, when he and I returned to his home, I'd ask him what was up with the crystal aesthetic all over the place. I enjoyed testing new styles as much as the next woman, but glass was highly breakable. Why use it as your primary construction material?

We walked through a stone channel slowly sloping downhill with the lights turning off behind us and others igniting when we got close. Rounding a bend, we came to a big open cavern that had to be at least a football field across. The ceiling arched high overhead and spikes of clear blue much like the buildings these people lived in jutted down from the glassy light purple surface. Vines draped among the spires, covered with pale purple flowers. They also glistened in the light. More glass?

I was beginning to get worried about all this crystal.

Wind swept through the cavern, buffeting me with floral-scented humidity as I took in the numerous pools scattered across the base of the vast open room. Even the pool surrounds appeared carved from crystal. Did glass permeate the entire planet?

Blue-skinned aliens like Aizor sat in the water that, for now, looked normal enough to me, though it had a subtle purple tinge. Some bathed alone, others in groups, their animated chatter lifting through the air. A few were partly hidden by spikes of blue glass projecting up from the golden-brown soil underfoot, the soil flecked with purple flakes that reminded me of amethyst.

He led me to one of the empty pools, gesturing. "Wevire abreck."

"Water."

The grin he gave me made my heart skip a few beats.

Dangerous beast. I must back away.

This wasn't a sink to wash my hands, but it would do. I dipped my hand in, moaning at how perfect the temperature was. The water had an odd silkiness to it, but it didn't burn my skin or make me itch so far.

Perhaps it would be okay to use it for bathing. Hopefully, the water I drank last night came from a different—and colorless—source. If only there was a way to find out. Too many questions bubbled across my tongue. I wanted to shout them out, but Aizor wouldn't understand.

Without further ado, Aizor untied his loincloth, tossed it aside, and climbed over the side, settling in the pool. He sent me a grin that made my insides heat up and tapped the water with his palm, muttering a string of words I couldn't follow.

I understood his seductive tone very well.

Take off your clothing, pretty mate, and join me.

CHAPTER 10
AIZOR

My mate frowned and started to chatter. I didn't understand a word she said, but her tone could not be mistaken.

She was irritated with me. How was that possible? The sun shone outside, we'd exchanged some words in our languages, and we'd soon fill our bellies with wonderful food. For now, she was being invited to bathe with her mate in the soothing waters brought forth by our gods. What could be better than this?

Her lips compressed, and she linked her arms across her chest. I'd already noted that she had two breasts instead of four. I savored the unusual and glorious differences between our species.

"Come into the water. Wash. You'll feel happier," I purred. The water contained properties that relaxed both the body and mind. Surely, she'd appreciate this as much as my people.

She continued to scowl. I'd already seen my mate

could be . . . surly. Perhaps once she'd had multiple amazing orgasms, she'd feel better.

I expected her to pivot and stride away, but she surprised me, stepping into the pool—fully clothed.

"You don't need to wash your clothing," I said as she dropped onto a seat opposite mine. "While we share tasks in my clan, our gods take care of most." Once she felt settled, she'd take her turn with the tasks our gods ignored, just like we all did.

She gasped and dipped her hand into the water, lifting it and frowning down at it while rubbing the pads of her fingers together. Her burst of excited sounds echoed around us, drawing the attention of those nearby. They smiled. A few sent me approving looks. Then they all returned to their bathing or conversation.

The pools were a place we came to not only to get clean but to allow the emollient in the water to relax us. It made a few of us feel giddy.

And as some also knew, it could prove arousing.

Shooting me a grin, she sloshed around in the water, rubbing her arms and sighing. While her hands continued down her front and even across her back where she could reach, I leaned against the wall of the pool, spreading my arms across the top to watch.

She paused and lifted her arm, displaying our mating mark. But no matter how hard she rubbed it; it wouldn't come off.

"Why do you wish to remove it?" I asked, but she only huffed and grumbled.

Yes, surly.

With a sigh, she returned to cleansing her body.

I enjoyed watching her stroke herself, though I'd prefer to do it for her. My largest cock thought so too, thrusting against my abs in growing excitement.

She continued gliding her hands all over her body while spilling joyful-sounding words from her mouth. After releasing her hair from the tight, spiraling band it had been secured in, she ducked below the surface, getting it wet. When she rose again, it hung in dark tendrils around her shoulders. She rubbed it, which wasn't as stimulating as watching her stroke her dual breasts, but she was enjoying this so much, I could do nothing but grin.

Waving around and splashing at the water, she continued to talk. If only I could understand what she said outside of our home.

I eased around the pool to sit closer to her.

She edged away from me, giving me a stern look and releasing words that made it clear *she* could touch her body, but I could not.

My heart spasmed to think she didn't want to be near me, to touch me. But pushing her didn't appear to be helping. Perhaps if I treated her as a friend for now, she'd soften to me.

While I'd promised to ask the gods about sending her back to her world, that didn't mean I wanted her to leave. I'd do all I could to convince her she belonged here with me.

She continued to rub herself. I stared, overcome with how lovely she was, especially when wet. The water made her skin glow, and while it wasn't blue, I was coming to adore the paleness and the way tiny spots of brown teased across her upper cheeks and nose.

Eventually, she finished stroking her body, praise the gods. My cock couldn't take much more visual stimulation.

She waved her hand to where I'd dropped my loincloth, now absorbed into the ground like many items we'd been gifted with, and we got out of the pool. I collected drying cloths for us both, plus clean clothing, knowing the ever-watching gods would ensure whatever I gave her fit despite her tiny size.

She stood beside the pool, water dripping from the long tendrils of her hair and from the hem of her tunic that clung to her frame. I adored the things that made her so different from a Zuldruxian, like her two breasts instead of four and her dark hair shot through with sunshine that was far different from the pure silver of my people.

I'd never seen anyone prettier than my new mate, and I was struck anew by her beauty, by how perfectly formed she was in a unique way that only made her more special.

She was my mate, and I cherished her already.

My large cock kicked against my abdomen, telling me it appreciated how gloriously pretty she was as well. It begged me to take her back into the pool and set her on my lap. I could lift her and drive her down onto my shaft, claim her like Tepesta's mate was loving her body in one of the more secluded pools on the opposite side of the cavern. Only the rhythmic slosh of water and their stifled groans gave them away.

Because I sensed my mate wasn't eager to expose her body to me or anyone else, let alone ride my cock, I urged her over to the wall and held up a large drying cloth, blocking her from view—even my own. She sent me a look of gratitude that made my heart flounder, then quickly removed her wet clothing, dried her body, and dressed in the tunic the gods had produced while we were in the pool, one crafted of deep blue cloth with gold trim.

Pinching the material away from her body, she made soft, sighing sounds punctuated with words I took for pleasure.

What sounds would she make while I plunged my cock—or my tongue—inside her?

She quickly crafted a long, thick weave with her hair, locking it away once more rather than allowing it to fly free. She blotted water from the tip with her drying cloth. Looking up at me, her smile grew big enough to make my heart explode. I swallowed hard, mesmerized by her animation and the fact that I'd given her joy. She chattered gaily and even leaned forward to pat my chest in a way I could only take as affection.

That's when I noted that her hands were as tiny as the rest of her, only half the size of my own.

"Mate," I said with worry.

Pausing, she cocked her head.

"We'll soon find pleasure together." Pray to the gods this was so. "I'm . . . concerned."

Her frown only deepened.

"One of my cocks is very big."

Someone snickered in one of the pools behind us, and I shot a scowl over my shoulder. Whoever it was shut up fast, and I turned back to my mate, leaning close to speak only for her.

"Will my biggest cock fit inside your tiny body?"

CHAPTER II
VANESSA

Maybe Aizor wasn't such a bad guy after all. He'd been a true gentle-alien, creating a shield for me to dress behind with the stone wall at my back.

The tunic he'd brought me must've been made for a Zuldruxian child because it fit well. I belted it in like Tapesta had with a matching strand of gold, marveling at how lovely the Zuldrux clothing was. The outfit even came with cute gold shoes that were much comfier than they looked.

Clean and refreshed, I walked with him out of the cavern, studying the dark purple stone walls and the tiny sprigs of golden vegetation growing up through the cracks. A few of the plants bloomed with pink, purple, and gold flowers.

To think I might be the first human to see the plants on this planet. If I was into botany, I'd start a journal, drawing each plant and writing down the names in the Zuldruxian language.

Hold on. I came to a skidding halt. Aizor kept walking but stopped as well, looking back. He spoke, and I felt irritated that I couldn't understand. His meaning was more or less clear, however.

Why did you stop?

"I stopped because, for just a moment, I realized it might not be horrible to be stuck on this planet." Thank the aliens (I couldn't say gods) that he *didn't* understand.

I caught up and walked beside him. He sent me the sweetest smile.

He was much too appealing. Warmth swirled low in my belly and shifted downward, pooling between my legs. I hadn't thought he could look better than last night with all his miles of smooth blue skin and wearing only a scrap of fabric covering his cocks. After his bath, he'd dressed in dark brown pants and a vest with ornate stitching along the edges, giving him an almost Egyptian appearance I found incredibly sexy. With his silver hair fluttering around his strong face in the light breeze, this guy was completely, utterly devastating.

Another thing that upset me.

I didn't want to find potential here, not in the vegetation and definitely not in Aizor.

We exited the cave, striding out into the sunshine. A few Zuldruxians walked around in the open area between the circle of glass homes. Were they truly made of glass? They couldn't be or they'd shatter. I'd examine Aizor's home when we returned. I was curious, if nothing else.

Instead of heading in that direction, he took me left,

continuing along the trail we'd taken to reach the bathing pool cave. The path wound around the side of the big hill.

We approached yet another crystal building, this one larger than all the others, and taller, with spires shooting at least three stories into the sky. While the majority of the structure was made up of various shades of blue, the taller spires gleamed pale silver in the sunlight. Truly, it was an amazing sight, and I stopped to gape at the beauty.

"I wish I understood how your world was built," I said. "Did the crystals grow here or . . .?" I couldn't imagine how they came to be.

Aizor stopped beside me. He took my hand and squeezed it as if he understood my question and thoughts. He spoke, but again, I didn't understand.

At my nod, we continued toward the big building and went inside. I stopped again to admire the architecture from this angle. Open all the way to the top, the silver beams fed by sunlight arched down from the tall spires. The lower areas glowed like the rarest blue jewels.

"Is this a central building?" I asked, taking in the enormous firepit in the middle of the open area that had to be a few hundred feet across. No fire had been lit inside the rocks surrounding it, but a pile of crystalline wood had been stacked nearby, ready to be ignited. How could crystal burn?

Evenly spaced open archways led to rooms in three-quarters of the exterior walls, their glassy rooflines curving up to seamlessly meet with the silver crystal.

Someone shouted, and a knee-high, pale blue creature burst from one of the openings, followed by a male shaking a long wooden spoon. While he bellowed and gave chase, the spiky furred beast waddled around the fire pit and raced toward us as fast as its four legs could carry it.

Aizor grunted and pulled a blade from the sheath strapped to his side . . .

"No!" I leaped in front of him, placing myself between him and the creature that looked a bit like a blue cat with some spiky-furred porcupine mixed in.

The beast yelped and scurried around me, fleeing out the front doorway.

Aizor lowered his blade and tilted his head, no doubt saying, *Are you out of your mind, woman? I nearly impaled you in the chest with my sword.*

"You can't kill it. It's a . . . Well, I don't know what it is but it's a sentient creature."

He huffed and returned his sword to its sheath.

The male who'd been chasing the creature paused beside us, barking out a bunch of guttural words, waving his arms and spoon around in an agitated way. He directed most of the conversation toward Aizor but kept shooting me scowls. With a twist of his lips, he stormed back to the room he'd exited.

Aizor tilted his head in that direction, and I tentatively followed. I glanced back, finding the blue creature peeking in through the opening. Its gaze met mine, and I swore I read thanks there.

I may have offended the guy with the spoon, but I'd made a new animal friend.

We walked into a decent-sized room with a long clear blue counter along the back wall. The spoon-waving male stood behind it. He glared at us before returning to stirring something in a big pot. I didn't see a burner beneath it but maybe heat radiated up through the counter like those glass top stoves everyone raved about.

Tables took up most of the room, and Zuldruxians sat, eating from, you guessed it, blue glass plates.

The shouting male scooped up food, placing it on a plate held out by the person waiting in the short line.

A cafeteria. Great. My belly scrambled, telling me to hurry up and feed it.

Aizor nudged his head in that direction, guiding me over to the counter where he lifted a plate and handed it to me, taking one for himself. We stepped in behind the last Zuldruxian and when it was our turn, he urged me to hold up my plate for a serving.

The Zuldruxian scowled but gave me a few spoonfuls. I lifted it and it smelled . . . interesting. I couldn't identify the brown lumps or the spices, but the gravy looked appealing. Shards of what looked like purple glass spiked through the food, but they couldn't be what they appeared.

Beyond the pans, Aizor paused. I waited with him, staring at the empty counter like he did.

A plate morphed out of the counter like it was some kind of 3D printer. Smiling and murmuring something that had to be thanks, though it sounded like *carcar*, he took the plate and juggling them both, urged me across the room to an empty table.

We placed our food on the glassy blue surface and sat.

Aizor dug into his meals with his hands and with a shrug, I did the same, delicately picking up a brown lump and popping it into my mouth. It was meat of some kind, and yummy. I munched through the tender chunk and moaned at the taste of the sauce that had a slightly spicy flavor. It was unlike anything I'd eaten before, but if this was an example of the food I'd be offered, I wouldn't starve.

But when I bit down on one of the purple crystals, I nearly broke a tooth.

Aizor crunched through his meal, smacking his tusks in a way that should be unappealing but instead was too hot to handle. Maybe it was the way his eyes glowed, such a Caribbean blue they made me want to gaze into them forever. Or maybe it was his groan as he savored the flavors.

All I could picture was him sinking his thick cock inside me while he groaned in exactly the same way.

CHAPTER 12

AIZOR

Van-eesa picked at her meal, eating the bits of roast bribard but leaving the shards of delicate purple vegetation we cultivated in a field not far up the hillside.

"You don't like the moobars?" I asked. She'd bitten into one but pulled it out of her mouth, setting it on the edge of her plate with a grimace.

She muttered something indecipherable, her cheeks growing pink.

I felt the same about our inability to understand each other. While I'd love to remain inside our home to ensure I understood her words, duties took up much of my daylight time. I was my clan traedor. My people needed me. Hopefully, she'd quickly learn more of my language.

When I reached for one of her moobars, she nodded, urging me with a wave to take them.

"Moobar," I said, lifting it.

She repeated the word. When she tapped on the edge

of the plate, I shared that word with her as well. She went from one object to another, pointing around the room, and after I'd given her our terms for at least twenty different things, she recited them correctly even if the words sounded slightly different.

She was clever. My earlier perception of her had been flawed. I was grateful once more to the gods for gifting her to me.

I pointed to the last bit of meat on her plate. "Bribard."

"Bribard." She popped it into her mouth and chewed, rubbing her abdomen and mumbling something in her own language.

Her tongue, so tiny and pink, appeared to have a difficult time with my language, but it was clear she was making an effort. The idea thrilled through me. Perhaps she wouldn't want to leave me after all.

She pointed to the few remaining strands of moobar on my plate and grimaced.

"You don't like them."

She shook her head and repeated her words.

"To quicken with my youngling, you need to eat a good diet. Meat alone will not be enough. We'll walk to the garden later today, and you can point out vegetation you might be willing to try instead."

She sighed, her lips thinning.

How could I please her? Pain stabbed through me, jumbling together with desire. Stark desperation made my shoulders slump. If the gods granted her request to return her to wherever she came from, could I go with her? It would be hard to leave my clan and the only home I'd ever known but losing her would be infinitely worse.

Though her body structure and appearance were so different from a Zuldrux, she was the loveliest being on this planet. Each time I looked at her, I couldn't stop drinking in the way her tiny nose curved up slightly on the tip, unlike the broad, thick noses of my own people. Her hair caught the light even inside, gleaming as if it had been spun by the golden upper portion of one of the crystal structures in the valley.

When I first saw her, I wasn't sure about mating with a female who only had two breasts, but now I couldn't stop staring at them. They jiggled, unlike those of the females in my clan. And I hadn't missed the ripe buds in the center surrounded by darker pink. How did Vaneesa's species nurse their young if they didn't have tubes projecting from the base of their breasts like a Zuldruxian?

I didn't care. Her differences only made her more appealing.

"Try this." I lifted a slice of the god-given fruit and offered it to her. She tentatively touched it with her tongue, and I stifled a groan. I needed to stop picturing that tongue on one of my cocks. Of her sucking like my smaller cock would on her clit.

Her eyes lit up at the flavor.

"It's fruit," I said.

"Mmm." She held my hand and bit off a good-sized chunk, chewing, her eyes gleaming brighter. I nudged the plate her way and watched with joy as she heartily ate everything on the surface.

"More?" I asked, waving to the counter.

She shook her head. No. At least the bobs of our heads matched.

"You need to know that I don't want to leave this place," I said. "It's the only home I've ever known. But for you, my mate," I swallowed down my dismay, "I would do it."

She frowned but didn't comment. But then, she didn't understand me. I wanted to gnash my tusks and bellow, but I sensed that would only repel her.

I reminded myself to be patient. I'd continue to teach her our words and slowly, we'd begin to understand each other when we were outside our home.

"After our meal," I bit down on and chewed through a spear of moobar. I wasn't hungry any longer, but we never wasted anything sent to us by the gods. "We'll take my hepadon to the valley to speak to the central gods."

She licked her fingers and sat back in her wooden chair, watching me as I finished her moobars. I'd poured her a mug of wellet, but she hadn't touched it. I nudged the drink closer to her, and she peered into the top, shaking her head before taking a tiny sip. She grimaced but drank the rest, probably to please me.

When it appeared she was finished, we left, leaving the structure to absorb the plates. They'd be renewed and returned when it was time for our next meal.

I took her to the evacuation building just in case, then back to the pools, though this time, we left the main channel and entered a small alcove on the right with a tiny pool just big enough for her to wash her hands.

She smiled up at me as we walked back out into the sunshine, and seeing her happy and knowing I was the cause, was a punch in the gut. It made my belly hurt, but it also felt amazing.

Taking her hand once more, I led her to the hepadon grazing area, the crunch of them biting off stalks of grass louder than the sound of our footsteps on the path. When we were close, I opened the gate and called for Voolon. Her head lifted and she snorted before trotting over to join us.

Van-eesa gasped and ducked behind me, seeking my protection as she should, though not from my tame hepadon.

I chuckled and dragged her forward to stand with me. "Be brave, my mate. Voolon will never cause you harm."

Voolon came to a halt in front of us, and I reached up to pat her snout. She nibbled playfully on my fingers before peering at Van-eesa. Her nose shot out to bump my mate's chest.

Van-eesa released another waaaa sound that must be her favorite saying.

Did she have similar pets where she came from? She must.

"Voolon is sweet," I said. "I raised her from the time she hatched from her egg." Later, I could take her to the hatching grounds, and she could pick out her own mount from the hepadon young. She'd raise it and train it to be gentle with her, though I didn't mind her riding with me. There was no better feeling than Van-eesa pressing her tiny frame against mine.

I took her hand and though she resisted, I placed her palm on Voolon's cheek. The hepadon nibbled it like she had mine. Van-eesa cringed, but she gave me a weak smile and patted the beast, quickly retracting her hand. She no longer released the *waaaa* sound.

"Up you go," I said, lifting Van-eesa and sweeping around to the side of Voolon to deposit my mate on the hepadon's back. Her eyes widened, and she gaped down at the beast who shifted but remained steady. A jump, and I mounted behind her. I tucked her back against my chest, lifting her onto my thighs.

My cocks announced they were eager for whatever might come next, the large one stiffening, the smaller one humming in tune with my heart.

Van-eesa wiggled and shot me a glare, muttering something I was grateful I couldn't understand.

When I urged Voolon forward with a nudge of my heels, Van-eesa latched onto my arm I'd wrapped around her waist. Emitting strangled gasps, she clung as the hepadon moved slowly past the edge of my village.

Once we'd reached the upper end of the trail weaving down the mountain and into the central part of the valley where the majority of the crystal gods lived, I urged Voolon to go faster.

Air rushed past us, sweet with floral perfume, the pungent aroma lifting off the needle trees now that the sunlight had hit them. I sucked in a deep breath, grateful all over again that I had the chance to live in this world during this time, that I had a healthy clan waiting for me at home, a sturdy structure to sleep in at night, plus the care of our gods.

And my precious mate who I hadn't given up on yet. I'd do my best to prove to her that I was worthy, and she'd soon welcome me with open arms.

As Voolon went faster, her paws thundering on the rough ground, Van-eesa shouted out her favorite word.

Grinning, I echoed it. "Waaaa!"

CHAPTER 13
VANESSA

I'd always thought horseback riding would be fun. But shifting on the spine of a galloping, blue crystal triceratops while Aizor's cocks rubbed against my ass? It should be a total turn-off—but it wasn't.

His main cock was enormous. Thick. I shouldn't find anything about this guy appealing.

Yet I did.

I kept wiggling, trying to ease away from him only to find the jarring pace grinding my body against his.

His main cock got harder. I couldn't tell if the smaller one got erect as well, but a subtle hum vibrated against me.

Slickness bloomed between my legs.

As the creature the size of a travel trailer rushed down the mountainside, Aizor held me snug against his chest. Since he wasn't jarring in every direction like I would if I rode alone, and he was taking us somewhere, I did my best to relax. To ignore how turned on I was by bouncing around on his lap.

I tried to focus on the world around me because it was gorgeous, from the crystal trees in varying shades of purple, to the exposed ground made up of gold flecked with lavender stones, to the way the dewdrops on the spiky grasses sparkled in the sunshine.

Aizor groaned, and I knew why. He wasn't admiring the view; he was getting aroused by my body rubbing against his own.

With all the movement, his arm had slipped up, a thick band across my breasts. And with each rolling jostle, his arm rubbed. My nipples hardened to pebbles, and Aizor's low groan rang out behind me again.

This was completely fucked up, but I couldn't hold myself back. One wave of arousal was followed by another, each driving me toward the elusive peak.

And curse me forever, but when his hand slipped along my thigh, I moaned and ground my ass against his cock.

He bunched up my tunic, exposing my lower body to the cool air, then his fingers dove between my legs. They wrangled through my wet folds in a way I should find offensive but didn't, before he latched onto my engorged clit and rolled it.

Fuck, fuck, fuck.

Too far gone to do anything but pulse my pussy against his hand, I tipped my head back against his chest and whimpered with need.

He drove a finger inside me while another continued

to tease my clit. And he rocked his hips against my back, growly and snapping his tusks in my ear.

When he added more fingers, I started thrusting as best I could while the beast below us continued galloping down the hillside. Aizor's groans grew heavier, deeper, and that turned me on even more.

I bucked, riding his hand while he guided the crystal triceratops along the wide trail at a rolling pace that only thrust his fingers deeper inside me.

My orgasm crashed over me all of the sudden, blasting me into the outer atmosphere as if I rode a mechanical bull with my hand in the air, a scream erupting from my throat, and my pussy igniting.

He shouted, and his body shuddered behind mine.

Wetness spread across the back of my tunic, but I was too into riding the waves to care.

Finally, I came back to the ground.

Aizor tugged his fingers through my folds and across my clit, making me shiver all over again. He lifted his hand and examined the slick juices coating it, before he sucked me off his fingers, groaning once more.

It didn't take long for the heat of embarrassment to climb into my face. I felt scalded with it. Here I was, begging him to help me go home, plus insisting I wasn't his anything, and he'd just given me one of the best orgasms in my life.

One of them?

Alright, the best.

I had no clue what to make of it.

The air was crisp yet not overly chilly, even while we

moved at a rapid pace. And Aizor's arm felt warm and comforting around me now that my body had blasted to the stars and back.

I wiggled, tugging my tunic back down over my thighs, and stared blankly at the vegetation, the ground, and the sky, trying to ignore what we'd just done. At least no one had seen us—I *hoped* no one had.

If I had to be abducted and sent to a distant planet to become an alien's bride, this wasn't such a horrible place to wind up in. I could've done a lot worse. Heaven knows that when a woman is kidnapped, the scenario rarely turned out right.

Once he'd done feasting on my wetness coating his fingers, he started pointing to one thing after another, shouting what it was called, as if me learning how to converse with him would make all the difference.

I dutifully repeated the words, sliding them into the library within my mind. I didn't have a photographic memory—if only—but being in college had sharpened that part of my brain. Would I remember all the words? Not a chance. But if I remained here much longer, I would slowly learn to speak his language.

And where would that leave me? I still wanted to return to Earth. I had a good job, a nice apartment, and friends.

There wasn't anything for me here.

Except Aizor, a tiny part of my mind suggested.

"Fuck off," I told it.

"Fook eff?" he asked.

"Yeah, that's it. Fook eff."

"Fook eff," he shouted as if it was my name and he'd miraculously learned it.

My laughter burst out, a tad hysterical, but a real laugh all the same. Aizor's chuckle grew in volume until we were pretty much rolling around on the back of the beast. I couldn't imagine what it must think, assuming it contemplated more than where its next meal of crystal grass was coming from.

We'd orgasmed together on its spine and now we were freaking out and shouting *fook eff*.

We reached the bottom of the mountain, and the land leveled off. The trail continued, wide enough for two of the beasts we rode on, though we met no one else along the way.

If I was stuck here forever, would it be *that* bad to stay with Aizor? I'd always wanted to get married and have kids, though not with my controlling ex. Aizor had a nice sense of humor, he was treating me kindly. He'd talked about massaging my feet. And let us not forget the way he'd just finger fucked me.

A woman could do a lot worse than wind up with him.

"Don't think about stuff like that," I whispered.

Aizor leaned close and delivered a long string of smooth words by my ear, but I didn't understand a thing he said. That made me sad. Maybe he was telling me how much he admired my appearance in the Zuldruxian tunic or how he'd enjoyed licking me off his fingers. I wanted to know that if it was the case.

Hand gestures and knowing the meaning of the food we'd had for breakfast would only take me so far.

Crystal structures jutted up from the center of the lush valley ahead. They'd been built—formed? —on an island surrounded by an enormous lake. Did the triceratops swim? If so, what lurked in the light purple, hopefully not dangerous, water?

Aizor parked his beast near the shore and slid off, taking me with him. He put me on my feet and stared down at me, studying my face and my chest. I'd already noted the dual versus four boobs thing and wondered what he thought about that. Mine were big—too big, actually—but for the first time since I was twelve and they'd started to sprout, I felt boob-deficient. How many children did Zuldruxian women have at one time to need four? It was a good thing multiples didn't run in my family.

Although, his spermies might have a different idea.

"Argh," I growled. "Stop thinking about his sperm."

"Spoom," he said, frowning at my arm. Yeah, that's what it was called.

I did appreciate that he was making an attempt to learn my language or what he thought was my language.

I was going to ask him what our plans were next when he lifted me to his eye level.

He grinned so sweetly; I couldn't hold back my own smile. My body felt deliciously languid, and this guy was to blame.

And then he kissed me.

CHAPTER 14
AIZOR

As I kissed Van-eesa, desire pounded through me. I couldn't get the memory of her taste off my tongue. She'd responded sweetly to my fingers and after, when I licked off her juices, I nearly came all over again.

My main cock responded to her kiss, thrusting my loincloth up into the air. My mate was softening to me. Perhaps she was reconsidering her wish to return to wherever she'd come from?

When she wrapped her arms around me, spearing her fingers through my hair, my body caught flame. I was hers and hers alone, and I wanted to shout it out to the world. Make sure everyone knew she was mine.

I thrust my tongue inside her mouth, finding her tiny pink one, and a groan erupted from inside me. While Voolon shuffled her paws nearby and dropped her head to graze, I lowered my mate to the spiky grass and climbed over her, caging her upper body with my arms.

I deepened my kiss, angling her head to reach every bit of her mouth.

And when I cupped one of her breasts that was infinitely softer than the firm texture I'd found with a Zuldrux female, 1 almost exploded against the front of my loincloth.

Then my mate smacked my shoulder, her hit no harder than a youngling flailing its tiny fist.

I lifted my head, and she released a string of words I didn't need an explanation of. Her scowl gave it away. Lifting myself off her, I sighed and tugged her up as well.

She stepped away from me and huffed.

It was going to take more persuasion to convince my mate we were meant to be together. At least I was patient.

She stomped back and forth in front of me. I admired her beauty that was vastly different from my own people's norms yet gorgeous all the same.

A crack of a stick in the woods to my left made my smile drop and my body go on alert. I spun with my sword lifting, scanning the woods but not seeing any movement. However, the forest stretched for many varns, and the Celedar Clan made their home there. Nevarn was a crafty traedor, and it would be unwise to show him anything but a strong front.

I snarled in case anyone might be near enough to hear.

Van-eesa froze, her wide-eyed gaze following mine to the woods. She sidled over to stand behind me, her palms pressed against my back. I chuffed; grateful she sought me for protection if nothing else.

After listening and hearing nothing for a long while, I lowered my spear, though I kept a tight grip on the hilt.

"Come," I said, waving to the island housing our higher crystal gods. "We'll cross."

Her gaze followed mine, but her posture didn't loosen. I suspected her world was much different than mine, making her justly frightened. She'd soon learn I'd protect her always.

While keeping an eye on the woods and my hearing acute, I took her hand and led her to Voolon, making sure the beast had enough grass to graze on while we were gone. Voolon would graze and wait for us to return; I didn't expect we'd be on the island for long.

Van-eesa asked something softly, still shooting sharp looks toward the woods.

I patted her arm. "Remain close, mate. I'll guard you from all harm. When we return to our clan, I'll arm you with weapons. You're completely defenseless unless you remain near me, and I have to hunt on occasion and handle duties for my clan. I want you to feel secure at all times."

She frowned up at me, gnawing on one of her blunted claws shaded bright blue. I'd wondered about them but hadn't yet had the chance to ask. Were they another sign that she belonged to the Indigan Clan?

I led her to the edge of the shore, approached the bribard bone mounted on a pole, and lifted it. Long ago, so far in my clan's past that no one knew when, it had been hollowed out and hung here for any of us to use. The island was neutral territory, as was the shore on this part of the lake. Anyone who dared fight here was quickly chastised by the gods. And no one would dare do more than behave with utmost reverence while they remained on the island. It was the central home of our gods, and the fates help anyone who broke the sanctuary of this solemn place.

I pressed one end of the bone to my lips and blew through it, creating a low, mournful sound that echoed across the water and within my bones. The first time I was allowed to use the bone to call a caipareel was one of my proudest moments. I was ten at the time, and that time stood out vivid in my mind.

Bubbles erupted in the water halfway between where we stood and the island.

"Eeep," Van-eesa said, backing away.

I took her hand and squeezed it. "Look, my pretty mate. Our caipareel has heard the call and comes."

She looked from me to the water, her mouth spreading wide. When she bared her teeth, I did so too. Perhaps this was a gesture her people used to welcome creatures such as the caipareel.

"*Fook eff,*" I bellowed in case her saying applied to this moment as well.

She snorted and her eyes watered.

I placed my sword in the sheath running down my spine where I could still pull it quickly if needed and turned her my way, cupping her face. I leaned close, studying her eyes that continued to water. Her face was flushed as well.

"Are you sick?" Stark, cold fear shot through me, and I swallowed hard. "If your eyes keep watering, I'll take you to the healer when we return home. He'll cure you." I suspected my fragile mate could be easily harmed. Look at how pale her skin was, not the rich blue of my people. And thin, so easily torn. I pinched a bit of it up off her arm, shaking my head.

I no longer worried she was defective, but my concern that her body was not made to survive our harsh world persisted.

Another thing to ask the gods about. Perhaps they could outfit her with some kind of shield that would prevent her from sustaining life-threatening injuries.

The caipareel approached beneath the water, pushing waves toward us. They crashed against my legs, and I grinned. There wasn't anything better than riding within a caipareel—except the feel of my mate riding my fingers.

When the caipareel erupted from beneath the water and towered over us, a bulbous mass of clear crystal exoskeleton and deep purple innards, I gave it a deep bow.

Van-eesa cried out and collapsed at my feet.

I'd passed out.

Me, who could look at blood and not feel a twinge. Who could probably gut a deer in a pinch and eat the heart raw. Who could clean up cat puke along with the best of them . . . had passed out.

Thankfully, I roused quickly because a clear crystal puffer fish the size of a small house and with sharp spikes jutting off its body and long clear fangs had erupted from beneath the water and was roaring toward us.

I leaped to my feet and yanked on Aizor's arm, trying to drag him away from the approaching beast. Was he stunned by the creature's appearance, or had it somehow lulled him? I'd seen no evidence of what I'd call magic in this world, but I'd only been here about twenty-four hours.

"Come on," I shouted. "We've gotta run."

When he just blinked down at me, looking puzzled, I

jumped and grabbed the hilt of his sword, wrangling it out of the sheath.

The mean daddy puffer slammed against the shore and skidded toward us . . .

I thrust myself between it and Aizor and growled, baring my teeth and struggling to lift the very heavy sword. Just try to bite me or my mate, and I'll . . .

Aizor plucked the sword from my hands and quickly returned it to the sheath. He swept me up, tucking me beneath his arm and rattled on about who knows what all in what I took as a chiding voice.

While I flailed and bellowed for him to put me down, he strode toward the puffer.

Its mouth opened.

Oh, shit. He'd decided to get rid of me. He was going to chuck me into the mouth and wash his hands of me, so to speak. He'd plea to his gods for them to send him a new, improved mate. One who could not only understand his language but who swooned on the bed furs.

When he patted me on the head and murmured something even I, in my wildly uncontrolled panic, could only take as reassurance, I stopped struggling.

While I gaped and cringed, he walked down the shore and stepped inside the creature's open mouth. He continued along the throat—please don't swallow! — until he reached what must be the stomach. Murky liquid sloshed at the bottom, and I didn't want to know what the floating blobs might be.

He slid me around and perched me on his waist with an arm around my back like I was an unruly toddler.

Then he chattered away in a soothing voice while the mouth of the creature closed.

It wiggled, backing into the water, and sunk.

I yelped and clung to Aizor while he patted my back, pressing my face against his shoulder.

When the creatures jostling smoothed, I cracked one eye to peek. We were floating below the surface inside a freaking alien puffer fish.

I sucked in a breath that oddly tasted sweet—definitely not examining that closely while partly digested gook sloshed around not far from my feet. I had no interest in asking him to put me down, but oh how I stared around in wonder.

Our puffer ride had clear flesh.

Fish of every imaginable color of purple zipped here and there, schools of them swarming in one direction then another. Some took one look at the puffer and bolted with a flick of their tails while others hung in one place, cocking one of many eyes our way. Spiky plants coated the bottom in various shades of pink, green, and purple, and tinier glassy fish darted around the strands.

The puffer undulated through the water, and I assumed it was taking us to the island.

The wonder of this place never ceased to amaze me.

I looked up to find Aizor grinning. He said something that sounded kind, ending it with *fook eff*. That got me laughing, and he joined it.

When his smile grew wider, my breathing came to a halt. Damn, he was gorgeous when he grinned. Even more handsome when he laughed. The skin around his Caribbean blue eyes crinkled, and his whole face glowed.

And when he leaned over and gave me a kiss, I melted.

Caught up in the wonderful feeling, I tightened my legs around him and stroked his face, opening his mouth to his tongue.

Everything inside me pounded as a mixture of lust and affection galloped through me. I clung to him, stroking his face, and tilted my head to give him better access to my mouth.

His tongue swirled across mine, and when he lifted his head, he stared at me with a look I could only describe as love. Like, he adored me for who I was and who I might be in the future. As if he couldn't imagine a world without me in it.

The same feeling crashed through me, and it scared the wits out of me.

I dragged my gaze from his, pressing my face against his shoulder, struggling to regain control.

Why was I thinking of my jerk of an ex and how he used to tell me I meant everything to him while checking out whatever woman happened to be walking by?

I bet Aizor wouldn't even notice if someone passed us as long as I was there with him.

Comparing him to a jerk only made him more appealing, and that scared me too.

"I—"

The puffer fish grounded on something hard, jolting

us forward, though Aizor barely shifted his feet in the yuck.

I bit back whatever I was going to say as the fish slowly turned to face our destination. Its great maw stretched wide, and Aizor walked up the throat slope and out into pure sunshine.

As the fish slid back into the lake, he walked into the water up to his knees, where he was swarmed by tiny fish who licked off every bit of the gook coating his gorgeous blue skin.

With a grunt, he walked back up onto the shore and placed me on my feet.

"There, my pretty mate," he said. "Wasn't that a pleasant journey?"

CHAPTER 16
AIZOR

My mate had been so stunned by my world, she'd collapsed. Perhaps she was seeing everything my clan and I could offer, and it had overwhelmed her with joy. Before I could lift her, hold her, she woke and rose to her feet, I swept her up and carried her into the caipareel. I'd enjoyed holding her while we traveled, and I hoped she'd allow me to hold her again soon.

When I placed her on her feet after emerging from the caipareel, she peered around in amazement. I entered the water to cleanse my legs and returned to her.

"I . . ." She stared at me, stunned. "We're not inside your home but I understand what you're saying."

I wasn't surprised. "This is a sacred place for us, some say the birthplace of our gods."

"You see your gods?"

"In everything they do, but as far as I know, they're not physical beings like you or me." I swept my arm to the center of the island where the tall crystal structures were clustered. "Some say the godly structures were here from the moment our planet formed, while others say they arrived here in ships much larger than yours. My clan elder believes the latter."

Because I was eager to speak with the gods and go home, I took her hand and led her along the path from the shore to the courtyard entrance.

"The stones on the path look like glass," she said. Stopping, she stooped down to touch one. "They're gorgeous. So many colors. They're much like mosaics I saw in a museum once except these are slightly rounded instead of flat. And they're smooth."

"Many have walked here before us."

Straightening, we continued on the path, her stopping to marvel at the vegetation growing on either side.

She pinched a branch on a tree covered with pink blossoms. "It feels almost like glass as well." With a snap, she broke the end of the limb. "Oh, oh."

I took it from her and licked it.

Her eyes widened and a low laugh bubbled up her throat. "It's edible?"

I nodded and kept licking.

Her eyes widened as she watched. "You have a very . . . thick and long tongue."

"You do not."

"I'm defective," she said with a low laugh.

"You're perfect. If I haven't made that clear, I want to do so this instant. You, my mate, are perfect just the way you are."

"Some guys would say they wished my tongue was long and thick as well."

I frowned. "Would that give you a better appetite for the delicacies of my world?" I handed her the twig, and she stared at it before licking it herself.

"I've died and gone to Wonka," she cried out.

"What is a wunka?"

"It's a movie. This is sweet. It tastes like cotton candy." She sucked on it, swirled her tongue around it, and at that instant, I understood what she meant about long, thick tongues.

"You can eat it," I croaked.

Her dual fluffs of hair above her eyes, something Zuldruxians didn't have, lifted. "What happened to your voice?"

I leaned close. "I was imagining a few places I could lick you and where you might use your tongue on me."

Her face turned the same color as the blossoms behind her. "We . . ." The fluffs dropped, as did her smile. She tucked the twig inside her mouth and crunched through it, turning to start walking again. "Let's go see your gods."

My words upset her. Did that mean she didn't want me licking between her legs? Females were confusing. I'd already determined this. But this female was the most puzzling of all.

I walked with her, though we stopped at the tall entrance.

She tipped her head back to peer up. "This is like a

big glass Disney-ish castle. The tree broke easily. Are the buildings just as fragile?"

"They wouldn't have lasted this long if they were." I rapped my knuckles on the surface beside the arched opening and it clanged.

"It sounds like metal." Leaning close, she ran her fingertips across it. "It's as smooth as it looks and as thick as any wall in a house back on Earth. So pretty. Every color from the rainbow is represented in this big oval structure."

"The outer walls and their spires are beautiful at sunrise or sunset, when the light hits them at an angle. I could bring you here sometime to see it."

Her face tightened. "Maybe." She stepped through the archway with me following. "It's gorgeous here. The open area in the middle of the round wall has to be the size of a couple of football fields. It's amazing."

"It is large." I wasn't sure what a *fout-bail feehld* was, but I didn't believe it mattered. "While the custom had stopped after the great disease swept across our lands, our clans now plan to gather here again each year to visit with each other and celebrate the gods' bounty."

"What disease?" She paused while crossing the open area where clans would set up tables to exchange goods during the gathering. Colorful, smooth stones covered the floor of this area as well.

I explained how many sickened, how most of the gods also died, and how our people were still slowly dying, though no longer due to the disease. How our clan leaders had come together and spoken to the gods, begging them to help us.

"You're saying you asked your gods for mates?" she said.

"With so few females being born and few clan members already, our people won't live many more generations without their help. So yes, we asked them. Begged them to help us, to send you to us."

She sighed and leaned against the outer wall of the central structure that was also enormous and many stories tall. The spires had inspired many poems that spoke of their greatness. Would my mate be interested in hearing them when we all gathered in our Indigan central area tonight?

"I still can't understand how asking your gods for help resulted in me being kidnapped and brought here."

"I'm sorry you were taken against your will."

"It's not your fault." Pain etched lines into her face.

"In some ways, it is. If we hadn't asked our gods for help, they wouldn't have taken you."

"I'm one woman. Please don't expect me to save your people."

"If you wish to have young with me, I'll welcome you with open arms."

She snorted. "I'm sure you will."

"But if you don't wish for young, there are herbs you can take to prevent a child."

"Forever?"

I joined her, leaning against the outer wall, my lower arm brushing against her shoulder. "I would love to hold my youngling in my arms, but I would never force such a thing on you. You've already been forced to come here, to be my mate."

"Do mates ever divorce?" She explained the concept.

Turning to face her, I stroked her hair. So soft. Her appearance stunned me all over again, and my heart squeezed beneath my ribs. She was gloriously beautiful and it would hurt if she ultimately rejected me. "True mates like us? No."

"You're saying I'd have no say in this?" she growled.

"Just like with having young, it is your choice to stay with me or not, but true matings are rare. More often, they're fertile. No one would ever consider ending such a relationship. But if you don't want to be with me, I'd never force you to do so."

"I appreciate you saying that." She gazed up at me with her lovely eyes. Tiny hairs sprung from the lids. Zuldruxians only had hair on the tops of our heads. I'd already noted she had strips of fluff above her eyes, plus tiny, fine pale hairs on her arms. I'd discovered wonderfully coarse hair between her legs as if her folds and sweet pussy hid behind a briar shield.

How would that hair feel to my tongue? Would it be soft like the hair on her head or barbed? It hasn't pricked my fingers, though.

My groan ripped out, a sound full of frustration and desire. I was eager to taste her everywhere, and she was equally eager to leave me.

She eased away from me, and I released her hair, letting it fall to drape across her shoulder.

"You wanted to speak with your gods?" she asked, the fluffs above her eyes lifting once more. I'd already noted she used the gesture when she was surprised, but it seemed to be part of an inquiry as well.

"They reside in this structure." I tapped the smooth crystal wall we'd leaned against.

"I'll admit, this place is incredible," she said. "Gorgeous. The colors." The awe in her voice was appropriate. We were near the gods. They'd be listening. She should be amazed by the beauty of their structures.

"The varying colors represent each of our clans," I said as I led her along the outer aspect of the central building. The entrance to the main god room was on the other side. "My clan, the Indigan, resides within the gods that are gifted with the colors blue and silver."

"That's the color of your buildings."

I tapped a place in the wall whose color perfectly matched. "Other clans live in crystal structures of red or gold, bluish green and white."

"How many clans are there?"

"Too many to count, though in this area? There used to be three but now there are four."

"Why four now and not before? I thought your gods had been here for longer than you remember, that your people were dying out."

"Nevarn, the traedor of the new Celedar Clan, lives in the forest along the lake. He did something horrible and was banished from the Dastalon Clan."

"What did he do?"

"We don't like to speak of it." I lowered my voice as if

the world was listening when actually, in this sacred place, only the gods would overhear. "He killed his mate."

"His true mate? Is it because she wouldn't give him a divorce?"

"She wasn't his true mate. I don't know why he did it, but it was a terrible crime. Since life is sacred here . . . How can it not be? We're a dying species. Each person is precious. He was banished rather than killed for the murder."

"Whoa." She peered around. "And you said he lives in the forest near the edge of the lake?"

"He won't come near us. Have no fear." He'd better not, or I might not see his life as sacred as his traedor had. "When he left, some of the males went with him, angered by the decision their traedor made."

"But he killed her."

"I've heard there were circumstances the traedor didn't understand, but that Nevarn wasn't allowed to speak of them."

"I can't imagine any reason someone would have to take the life of another."

"I don't either. We kill creatures but only to eat. And we thank them for the sacrifice they make to keep us alive."

"Does any clan hunt for the enormous fish that brought us to this island?"

"Never. The fish is called a caipareel and its species has performed this duty for us for longer than anyone remembers. We protect it and it transports us to and from the island." I cleared my throat. "Nevarn's is the Celedar Clan, and their god bestowed bluish green and white on them."

"You said they're a new clan. How would they have a god or colors if they've been here forever?"

"They discovered a god we hadn't known existed in this area. I don't know anything about this god, just that Nevarn's clan has one. My friend, Firion, is traedor of the Dastalon Clan, that of the sky warriors. Their red rivals the sky at sunset."

"That must be Nevarn's former clan." She peered up, but we couldn't see the sky through the top of the crystal structure. "How do they live up there? On ships?"

"They fly on great winged beasts and live on islands that float in the sky above the ocean."

"Why don't the islands fall?"

I shrugged. "Such is the way of the gods."

A shiver tracked through her, and she hugged her waist with her arms. "I'm not sure I'm eager to meet their flying beasts if they're anything like the caipareel."

"They're well-trained. They rarely bite."

"Where do the final clan live?"

"My friend, Xax, is the second to the traedor of the Ulistar Clan, the Zuldruxians living among plant gods."

Pausing, she frowned, wedging the fluffs above her eyes together, creating yet another gesture with a new, indiscernible meaning on her expressive face. "Plant clan?"

"They live inside large plants thrusting up from the ground that they grow from spores. This clan is very small and we've encouraged them to come live with us, but their traedor prefers to isolate them. He's refused to join us so far."

"Are their colors bluish green and white as well?"

I shook my head. "Gold. Glorious gold. Our worlds are similar, aren't they?"

"In some ways, though our islands only float on the surface of the water, not in the sky."

"And how do you keep them from sinking into the water?"

She frowned. "They're large land masses with bases that extend all the way to the ocean floor. They don't sink."

"And neither do the sky islands, though they don't have bases anchoring them to the ground or hooks for clinging to the clouds."

"I can't imagine anything like that."

"We could visit one day and you could see how they live."

"Perhaps." She tapped the wall of the central compound. "We use material similar to this, though it's quite fragile. It shatters under a heavy blow."

"Some crystals shatter as easily here, as you saw with the flowering tree. The grass our hepadons eat is also fragile. If one treads on it hard, it can be crushed."

"You eat some of the crystals."

"Don't you eat your trees and grass and the creatures that roam your world?"

"We do, but they're not made of the same material. I'm not sure how my body will respond to them."

"If I know the gods, though no one truly understands their ways completely, they'll have ensured your body can eat whatever we do."

"Hmm," was all she said.

We rounded the large central pillar, and I gasped in amazement.

A circle of structures—the "pod" Van-eesa must've been referring to—had been placed in this section of the vast room, the tops of the long cylinders nearly meeting in the middle.

A female like Van-eesa lay inside each one.

Van-eesa snarled and before I could ask her what she was doing, she grabbed my dagger from its sheath at my waist and raced toward the pods. When she reached them, she lifted my weapon and drove the hard crystalline tip down on top of the first pod.

A loud clang rang out in the room.

I *felt* the gods awaken around us.

CHAPTER 17
VANESSA

"Damn fucking crystal gods," I bellowed, smacking the top of the closest pod over and over with Aizor's dagger. The weapon just bounced off. The sharp end didn't even mar the surface. Even worse, the woman inside remained asleep. If her face wasn't pink, I'd think she was dead. "Open, damn you! Open!"

"Van-eesa," Aizor yelled, dismay clear in his voice. "You mustn't do this." He snatched the blade from my hand and held it high enough overhead I couldn't reach it.

That didn't stop me from jumping, trying to grab it again. "Give me a better weapon if this one won't work. Anyone got a sledgehammer?" Tears streamed down my face. "Don't you see? They're trapped inside these . . . awful things. Look at them. Look at them!" I collapsed on top of the clear roof of the closest one, gazing at the woman lying inside. She looked relaxed. Like she was sleeping beauty just waiting for her prince to come and give her a kiss to release her from this glass trap. "This is Talia. Or Maggie. I'm not sure which. But see her long black hair? She has beautiful brown eyes, and no one may ever see them again."

"You know these females?" he asked, walking around, studying each person lying on her back, dressed in the same sheer nightgown I was wearing when I arrived.

"I don't. Not really. They were on the ship with me that left Earth. When your crystal god woke me, it sent mechanical arms to carry me to my pod. I saw them then, also being carried to these pods. I only heard a few of them calling out to each other." I wiped the tears from my eyes and walked among the pods, pointing. "This is Maggie. She and Talia are sisters."

I couldn't believe they'd stolen this many women from Earth.

"They don't appear to be in distress," he said, coming over to stand with me, his hand dropping onto my shoulder. He rubbed, and he must be trying to give me comfort, but nothing was going to make me feel good about this.

"Not in distress?" I scowled up at him. "Would you like to be lying in a glass pod waiting for . . . who knows what?" Probably to be *gifted* to an alien. "What if there's an earthquake or a big storm? They could die inside these stupid things." I brought my fist down hard on the top of the one holding a woman with curly blonde hair. "I remember her, but I don't even know her name. There are eight of them here and other than Talia and Maggie, I don't know *any* of their names." Wait. "There was a red-haired woman . . ." I looked around, but I couldn't find her.

My knees gave out. I only remained upright because I clung to the closest pod. "She's gone. Is she dead?"

"I don't know," he said softly. "We could ask the gods to free these women."

She must be dead. The poor thing. "We'll *demand* they free them. None of these women deserve this." *I* didn't deserve this. I snapped my head around, but I didn't see anything that might be a god standing nearby to be screamed at. No statues. No altars. "Take me to your gods, because I have a few choice words I'd like to say to them."

"Please be respectful."

"I'll be as respectful as they were with me when they kidnapped me from my home and everything I loved."

His shoulders fell. "You loved someone there?"

I shook my head. "I had an ex-boyfriend, but he was a total jerk. I stole some of his money and ran away after he hit me."

A snarl ripped up Aizor's throat, and he tightened his big hand on his sword jutting up his spine. "I'll ask the gods to send me to your world, and I'll kill him. How dare he hurt you?" His fingers traced down my face. "No one will ever cause you harm again. I'll make sure of this."

"I appreciate your willingness to defend me, but he's back there and I'm here. There's no need to beg your gods for a ship to take you there to kill him. If you did something like that, you'd be arrested. They'd hustle you to Area 51 and conduct experiments on you."

"Why would they examine me in such a way?"

"Because you're not from Earth. My people have a bad reputation for doing things like that. Or we assume they do. On Earth, no one knows if aliens are real or not, let alone what the government does with one they happen to catch."

"I'll take you to the gods," he said. "And I *will* ask them how I can seek revenge for what your hex did to you."

He led me away from the women slumbering. Waiting for whatever might come next.

Aizor had treated me well so far. Spoiled me, if I was being honest. But no one should be given to a male without her consent. We weren't objects or pets.

On the far side of this enormous building, arched entries led to alcoves along the far wall. Back home, I'd think they were offices or places where they might store goods. Here? Who knew where they led? Maybe even to an alternate reality.

I was *living* the alternate reality.

He stopped outside the opening on the far right. "When the traedors gathered and decided to ask the gods to help save our people, we came here. Never in my memory has anyone been allowed to pass through this entrance unless they have urgent need of the gods."

"It's an open doorway."

"It only appears as such. When one of my people tried to enter, they were repelled."

"You mean like . . . they were shocked or something?" I wasn't sure about this now.

"They walked into a wall they couldn't see."

"Something invisible, then."

"I don't know that term."

"It means something physical that's there, but you can't see it."

"Yes, an invisible door. But when we decided to speak to the gods, a few of us were appointed to come here to plead with them. I was one of them."

Aizor had many admirable qualities. I could see why the traedors would choose him to join them in their quest, though I hadn't met anyone other than those within his clan.

"Then," he said, "the gods allowed us to enter the room. Inside, you'll find enormous blossoms."

I frowned, trying to picture what he meant. "Flowers?"

He nodded. "If the gods are willing to speak with you, you'll be absorbed within one of them."

I wasn't feeling the love for being absorbed into anything, but this might be my only chance to plead with Zuldruxian gods who I was beginning to suspect were actually a superior alien species instead. Not that I was an expert in things like that. I only went to church a few times when I was little, and I'd taken care of my own religion after that—which was almost no religion at all. Who was I to say that these beings weren't actual gods?

"You don't need to go inside, assuming the gods will

allow you entrance," he said. "You could remain out here while I speak with them for you."

I appreciated that he was willing to do this for me, but I was a big girl. I could handle it. "I'm jumping into a blossom. Is there anything else I need to know?"

He smiled, though it held a touch of sadness. "I already told you to be respectful. My only other suggestion is that you listen to what the gods have to say, that you don't just shout at them."

"I never shout."

He snorted.

"Does it hurt?" My teeth chattered already. Was I really up to this after being pretty much swallowed by a giant fish then regurgitated on shore?

"No. The gods are kind. Benevolent even."

So said the male who was gifted with a woman.

"Full speed ahead, then." I started toward the open doorway, but he took my hand and held me back, turning me to face him.

Then he cupped my face and kissed me.

AIZOR

I'd never get enough of her mouth, of her fingers roaming my chest. She moaned and leaped up, wrapping her legs around me as if she never wanted to let me go.

She tasted like the heegar cakes Jessia made on special occasions. Incredibly sweet with a subtle hint of spice.

My body caught fire, and I backed her against the wall, holding her up with my hands on her plump ass. I squeezed her cheeks while she thrust her hips toward me.

I was filled with a need unlike anything I'd felt before, and it centered solely on this female. I'd willingly die in her embrace as long as I could taste her like this forever.

I lifted my head, and seeing her eyes closed and the pure bliss on her face was too much. My groan ripped up my throat, and I kissed down her neck, nipping at her tender skin while she shivered in my arms.

The gods might be waiting but they could do so forever. All that mattered was this female and showing her pleasure.

When I stroked her breast through her tunic, she arched her spine and cried out. Her nipples, so unlike a Zuldruxians hardened, and I'd die if I didn't get to taste them.

I bunched her tunic up her thigh and she shifted her hips, her moans urging me to rip the fabric up and over her head.

Her luscious breasts were like ripe troolon fruits with hard nubs perfect for sucking. I shifted her higher and she clung to my hair, wrapping thick chunks around her palms, holding tight. Her head tipped back, and she pushed her body against mine with excitement. I nibbled down to her breast and ran my tongue across the bud.

She cried out, her back bowing to press her breast into my mouth.

While I sucked on the bud, she panted and tugged on my hair, alternating that with pressing against the back of my head to hold me at her breast.

She kept thrusting her hips forward, rubbing her wetness across my abdomen.

My main cock was a spear gouging against my loin-cloth. I wanted to release it, plunge it inside Van-eesa's welcoming body, but not here. Not now.

I longed to consume my pretty mate with a hunger

I'd never felt before. Desire clawed through me, desperate and aching.

Leaving her breast, I kissed across her rounded belly. I thrust her thighs up onto my shoulders and while she held on, I dipped my nose between her legs, sucking in her heady scent. The need to taste her overwhelmed everything else.

I stuffed my face deeper, rubbing my nose through her saturated folds, sniffing in her delicious scent while growling. She cried out and spread her legs wider, welcoming me to do whatever I wanted with her body. The fact that she trusted me with this, if nothing else, made pride roar through my chest.

I would make sure she found so much pleasure in this act that she would never want to leave me.

Dragging my tongue through her wetness, I stopped at the top, gliding my tongue in quick circles around her clit.

The hair I'd been curious about was scratching against my face. It tickled, and I adored the feeling.

She cried out in gasping jerks, holding my head tight to her body.

She arched her back against the wall, thrusting her pussy into my mouth, coating my face with her amazing juices.

I was lost in her. So deeply caught up in her that nothing and no one else would ever compare.

Growling, I licked and sucked on her clit. I slid a finger inside her, groaning at how wet her tight sheath was, how the soft walls cushioned my hand. She'd do this with my main cock, tightening around it, milking it while I rutted inside her.

Her flushed face was a painting of pure rapture, strained with the intensity of her emotions.

She splayed her legs wider, and I pushed two fingers deep, grinding them against her inner walls. She'd take my cock so well. I'd wait a lifetime for that moment, that exquisite joy I sensed only this woman would give me.

I sucked on her clit, relishing how engorged it was, how great her need was—one only I would be able to satisfy. She was delicious, pure perfection. If only I could stay like this, lost between her thighs while she moaned and made cute little demands in her own language, *fook meeee* being the most prominent. *Fook* had to be a positive term.

Her body began to shudder. Her clit tightened. I reached up and rolled the bud on her breast, tugging on it while she whimpered and gasped.

When I added a third finger, curling them deep inside her passage, quivers rippled through her frame. She sweetly sucked on my hand as she came, calling out my name while yanking on my hair. I'd gladly give it all to her only to hear her come in such a way every day of my life.

She collapsed forward, onto my back, and I held her, pumping my fingers slowly inside her while she slowly returned to my world.

To me.

CHAPTER 19
VANESSA

When Aizor eased his head out from between my legs and gave me a lopsided grin, my heart clenched tight. Damn but he was cute, all covered with my wetness and gleaming with pride.

"You taste amazing, my pretty mate," he growled. "I will never need to eat again as long as I can feast on your ripeness."

If a guy back on Earth told me this, I not only wouldn't believe him, but I'd also probably laugh.

But the sweet look in his eyes told me he one hundred percent meant it. And the greedy way he stuck that wonderfully long, thick tongue out of his mouth to lap up everything on his face told me he'd gladly lay me on the floor and start all over again.

He'd not only gotten me off, but he'd also taken great pleasure in doing it.

I wasn't sure what to think about that.

He shifted my legs off his shoulders and cupping my

ass in his big hands, lowered me to the ground. My tunic hung around my neck, and it didn't take long to spear my arms through the sleeves, tug it down around my thighs and return the golden belt to my waist. My underwear, lying shredded on the rounded glass ball floor, had seen their last hoorah. There'd be no stitching them back together again.

It was wicked of me, but I took a bizarre pleasure in the realization that wearing nothing beneath my tunic meant Aizor could wrench it out of the way and eat me out whenever he pleased.

Wouldn't want to starve the poor guy, now would I?

How long did it take to fall in love with someone? Surely more than a few days. Yet, here I was, softening to Aizor already. Conjuring up sappy dreams of us grinding away together on his furs each night and lounging in the hot pools during the days. Holding hands.

Having younglings.

"Ugh," I muttered.

"Ugh?" He was still licking his face. He'd added his fingers to his mouth, sucking off every drop of my orgasm. With his slick face and a cocky look in his eyes, he was devastatingly gorgeous. Like, I-may-not-be-able-to-resist-him-for-long gorgeous. I needed to talk his gods into sending me back to Earth before I fell for him completely.

"We should probably . . ." I flicked my hand toward the opening that still waited, assuming we'd be allowed inside. "Why do *you* want to talk to your gods?"

His gaze shot away from mine. Okay, keep your secrets.

"You're not going to ask them to keep me here, are you?" Frankly, I wouldn't blame him if he did. He was clearly lonely. He'd made it clear he wanted a mate between the furs. And he had a point that his people needed new blood if they were going to thrive.

"If you remain here, it's because you want to," he said. "I want to ask my gods to give you the gift of our language everywhere."

Aw, that was awesome. "It would be nice to be able to talk to you outside your home and here. To speak with everyone else." I could make friends. Maybe get a job or start experimenting with all the vegetation on this planet. Figuring out what was edible and what wasn't. Test new dishes. I could ask his gods to give me an air fryer. A wok. A waffle iron. And even a—

Hold it right there.

I wasn't staying here. I couldn't stay here. My life was on Earth.

But what kind of life did I truly have back in that town in the middle of nowhere? I had a decent job. My boss was a kind person. I enjoyed chatting with the customers. But my ex must still be stalking me. He'd get revenge when he found me. I barely squeaked by with my income, struggling to make ends meet while living in a tiny studio apartment. I'd starve if Franklin didn't let me take leftover food home from the diner.

But staying here? I didn't want to think about that.

"I need to focus on my goal," I said.

He nodded, and damn, but he looked incredibly sad now that I'd said it.

As we walked toward the archway into the room housing his gods, my knees rattled together.

I'd just had a massively wonderful orgasm courtesy of Aizor's mouth, and all I could think of was begging him to do it again.

Speak with the gods? Ask them to send me home?

How could I even be contemplating leaving Aizor?

CHAPTER 20
AIZOR

The doorway to the vault of the gods allowed us entrance. Inside, Van-eesa stopped and peered around.

I knew what her goal was—to leave me. And the thought made my heart ball up and ache. But did I want her here if she only wished to return to her home?

I'd have to trust that whatever happened would be for the best.

"I don't see any flowers," she said. "Just an empty room that looks larger than it should be considering it's built against the back wall."

"This is the god's space. It . . . isn't part of my world, I don't think." I wasn't sure how I knew this. "As for the flowers, you'll see. Walk out into the middle of the room and wait. It's not frightening, though I'm sure you must be scared. Trust in them. They'll keep you safe. They won't cause you harm."

"Alright." She tugged her hand from mine and walked away from me.

Stark desolation ripped through my lungs, but I wouldn't hold her back. I wouldn't cling. Instead, I swallowed and stepped forward myself, waiting.

When the blossom erupted from the floor, encasing me, my only thought was for my mate.

Her scream rang out, and I snarled, struggling to break free of the gods' hold. I needed to reach her, protect her. I bellowed out my dismay.

The blossom clung to me and pulled me down, down, spinning while wrapping me in darkness bleak and empty. I couldn't tell if my eyes were open or closed. Finally, the whirling halted.

Why have you come here, Aizor? Are you not happy with your mate? As before, the god spoke in my mind.

"Let me go. I need to protect her."

"She is safe. Speak to us. Tell us what you need, why you have come to us again."

"I adore Van-eesa," I said. "Love her." I'd never think of lying to our gods. They saw all. Knew everything.

Trust, I reminded myself, struggling to control my heart rate. I wanted to go to her and hold her, make sure she didn't feel scared. But the gods would not harm her. I knew this in my soul.

You love her, yet you brought her here to plead with us to send her back to her wretched planet.

"Isn't it wonderful there? That's what I assume. It must be. She loves it. She aches to return to her former life. It must be the most amazing place; one I could only dream of."

Nothing can compare to Zuldrux.

"Our home *is* perfect. This is true." Pain stabbed through my chest at the thought of never seeing her again, never touching or tasting her again. "While I would give anything to keep her here with me, I'm asking you to send her back if this is her wish."

And this is why we gifted her to you.

"A gift should be given, never forced."

I sensed the gods were not happy with my statement, though if they had emotions, they'd never showed them. *She's your true mate. We searched to find her. Brought her for you.*

"I can't force her to stay here with me." No matter how badly it hurt, if she chose to leave, I'd smile and stroke her cheek and wish her well. Then spend the rest of my days mourning her loss.

We'll consider this. Is there anything else you need? Surely you didn't come here today merely to express your love for your mate.

"I want to seek revenge on her hex for hurting her."

That is not possible.

"Why not?"

Do not ask again. You will remain here on Zuldrux.

I didn't like this, but I must respect the will of our gods. "My final request is for you to give her the gift of understanding."

If she can only communicate with you inside your home,

this gives you a chance to show her why she belongs here with you.

"She wants to speak with everyone, not only me. If she remained here, her life would hold more pleasure and joy with complete understanding. She could make friends, hear the wise words of our elder. Speak to me when we're outside our home."

We will consider this. Is that all?

There was so much I could beg for, every bit of it wrapped up in Van-eesa, but I wouldn't ask for anything she didn't wish to grant me with love in her heart.

"I have no further requests," I said.

Then our conversation is over. Go with strength, Traedor Aizor. We acknowledge your trust and will reward you for it.

And just like that, I was spit out of the flower. I landed on my chest on the floor and skidded across it.

Then I rose and waited for my mate to finish speaking with the gods.

CHAPTER 21

VANESSA

I yelped when something erupted from the floor around me, bright purple segments snapping out then wrapping me in a cocoon, binding me while yellow and pink fluff exploded over my head. I was being mummified, and there was nothing I could do about it but scream.

A blossom, huh? This was a pastel nightmare.

Aizor bellowed my name, and I wanted to go to him, tell him I was okay, that I'd survived this like I had so many other things in my life. But I plunged down, down, away from him, and landed hard, the vibration jarring up my spine. I was absorbed in darkness and couldn't see anything around me. For a moment, panic shot through me, and a scream rushed up my throat. I could barely hold it back.

Be still. The voice echoed around me, reminding me of the one that woke me on the Mars spaceship.

"Someone's inside my mind," I cried out. "Get out of my head!"

How else will I speak to you?

Speak to me, not *with* me. I noted that. "You could use a mouth."

Which I don't have.

I thrashed, trying to break free of the bindings. "Then make one. Surely someone who can direct robocops to kidnap a bunch of women, steal a spaceship headed for Mars, and bring the women to an alien planet can create lips."

If you don't hold still, I'll make you.

The thought of mechanical claws bursting through the mummy-blossom and pinning me in place made me stop struggling. My feral panting echoed around me, and my heart rate thrummed in my ears at a furious pace.

"Send me home," I said, reluctantly adding, "Please."

This is your home.

"No, you stole me like I'm some kind of pet. You brought me here and gave me to an alien as if I have no free will of my own."

Few have any say in their lives.

"That doesn't make it right. You didn't ask if I was okay with your plan."

Would you have agreed?

"I doubt it."

We're giving you and the others the gift of language.

A jolt shot through my brain like I'd taken a blow to the side of my head.

"Ow." With my arms bound to my sides, I couldn't rub my aching temple. "Thanks?"

Return with Aizor to your home. Love him. Bear his younglings.

"I'm not a broodmare."

These people are dying.

"You can't pin that on me and a few women. Species die out all the time." The thought of the Zuldruxians fading away was a knife gouging my throat. Aizor, Jessia, who I'd only briefly met, and baby Willire and her mom, Tapesta. Each person had touched my heart already. "Save them."

We cannot do this on our own. We need you.

I'd never had a purpose in life, but there was no way they could expect us to save them.

If they die, so shall we.

"Are you saying you have a symbiotic relationship with the Zuldruxians?"

To some extent, yes. We came here so long ago; we've forgotten where we came from. We were welcomed. Worshipped. We wish to be revered once more.

"And you think forcing women to come here and hook up with Zuldruxians will make us love you like they do?"

We don't need love.

"Everyone does." The silence dragged on for so long, I had to break it. "Free the other women. Please."

When it's their time.

"It's not fair to keep them frozen like that."

They're safe. Healthy. They wait and they dream.

"They're probably having nightmares."

We don't dream.

I felt a twinge of pity for these alien beings who were entrenched in this planet and dependent on the Zuldruxians for worship, but my sympathy for them didn't shove aside my anger at what they'd done to me and the other women.

One week, the alien being said.

I stilled, waiting before blurting out, "One week for what?"

If, after one week, you wish to return to your wretched, dying planet—

"Hey, we have tacos and coffee, things I'll point out are *not* on the menu here."

—then we will return you.

My breath caught. "Really?"

You doubt our ability to do this?

"No, but I'm questioning *why* you'd do it."

We're not without feelings.

So far, I'd seen no evidence of that. But I'd be foolish to point that out or disagree.

We only ask that you give Aizor a chance.

A big part of me wanted to. "I can do that."

On the seventh day, come to us if you wish to remain here. If you don't come, we'll assume you want to return to your planet and will send you back.

That seemed reasonable.

"It's a deal." I could stick it out for a week. "Will you tell Aizor?"

Why would we?

Because they were Team Aizor, not Team Vanessa.

The thought of going home didn't make me as excited as I'd thought it would, because leaving meant saying goodbye to him.

"I'm not falling in love with him," I pointed out.

Silence.

I muttered, trying to fill the gap. "He has an amazing tongue. He's sweet and kind. He's a good person. But love takes time. It takes . . ." Trust.

I sighed, realizing I'd been pinning my general lack of trust for men on Aizor. He didn't deserve that.

Give us your answer in seven days.

"Alright."

Before I could ask them anything else, the blossom shot upward and spit me out onto the floor. Aizor rushed over and scooped me up in his arms. He dropped onto the floor beside the wall, placing me on his lap. After weaving my legs around his waist, he wrapped me up in his embrace.

It felt good to be close to him, to take the comfort he readily offered.

"What did they say to you?" I finally asked.

"That they'll give you and the other women the gift of understanding. And you?"

"I asked to go home."

He didn't tense up, per se, but I sensed his hearing suddenly sharpened. "Yet you're still here, as are the other women in the outer room. I looked."

"Your god told me my home is here."

"You don't agree."

"When I got here? No."

"And now?"

"I'm . . ." I looked up at him, and the hope in his eyes made my breath catch. I wasn't sure what I felt about this alien, but I didn't want to hurt him. If I did, it would shred my heart. "They told me they'll return me to Earth in one week if I still wish to leave."

"I have seven days to convince you, then."

Unlike when I first arrived here, he didn't sound cocky. He also didn't sound confident.

"Yes, seven days. I'm," I sucked in a breath and my hands actually shook, "I'm going to give us a chance."

He cupped my cheeks and tipped my head back, making me look up at him. "A male can do a lot in a week."

I couldn't hold back my smile. "A male can."

"Be prepared, mate."

My smile grew wider. "For what?"

"For me to show you why you want to remain here with me before the seven days are over."

My pulse surged, and my core throbbed. What would it be like to stay here forever as his mate? The thought scared me. I'd only been here a short time. It was okay to feel frightened. This wasn't just about being an alien's mate but adapting to a completely new way of life.

But . . . I was going to give it a shot.

And then, in seven days, I'd either come here and tell the crystal gods I wished to stay or they'd return me to Earth.

CHAPTER 22

AIZOR

"I hate leaving them," Van-eesa said as we walked again through the open room with the pods containing the other women.

"They're safe here."

"Are they?" Her hand remained on the top of one of the long cylinders as she looked my way.

"No one would dare challenge the gods to cause them harm."

"But one of them is missing." She peered around frantically. "The red-headed woman."

"Perhaps . . ." Yes, I would say it. "Perhaps she has been sent to her mate like you were."

"We need to find her. Help her."

"She could be anywhere on Zuldrux."

Her shoulders curled forward. "I hope she's okay."

"I could send some of my males to study the area, see if they can locate her."

"Would you?" Hope bloomed in her voice.

"I will."

She squeezed my hand. "Thank you."

"Of course. Are you ready to leave?" I had many plans for the next week. Seven days was not long, but it was better than no days. Could I convince her that she belonged with me for a lifetime?

"Yes, I'm ready to go."

We walked back down the path to the shore, and I blew through the bone, summoning a caipareel. I held my mate in my arms as it graciously gave us a ride back to the opposite shore. At first, Van-eesa appeared pensive, which was a change from surly, though I wasn't sure whether this was a good or a bad sign. I didn't want to ask what was bothering her, though I suspected she was worried about the other woman.

And about remaining with me.

What if she told me she couldn't wait for the seven days to end, that her only goal was to return to her home planet sooner?

We left the caipareel and it eased back into the water, disappearing from view.

Van-eesa watched it go, and when her smile rose, so did mine. "I still can't believe we rode in a giant puffer fish's belly."

While I understood her words, I also didn't. Poof-a fish must be a creature from her home world. Did any of her males rival a Zuldrux warrior?

"We'll return to my clan." I scanned the woods surrounding the lake but saw no concerning movement. Voolon watched us approach, and she didn't appear tense. But I couldn't shake the feeling we were being watched. The sooner I got my mate home and safe among my clan, the better.

Then I could work to win her love.

"If nothing else, I'm grateful I understand your language now," Van-eesa said. "Your god slammed the side of my head, which either knocked some sense into me or changed something in my brain."

"Did you need sense knocked into you?" I asked with a chuckle.

Her laugh joined in. "I might've."

I was grateful she appeared happy about this. Something had changed, and I welcomed it.

I lifted her onto Voolon's back and leaped up behind her, nudging my hepadon to turn and begin the journey home. She soon loped along the path weaving back up the mountain, leaving the valley and my uneasy feeling behind. By the time we reached my clan's territory, the sun had slid down to hover above the horizon. It would be dark soon.

"Are you hungry?" I asked. She must be. I was famished.

"Yes. What's for dinner?"

Even in this, she sounded happy. Had the gods found a way to bring about this change of heart? If so, I'd thank them until my dying day for whatever they'd said.

"I assume we'll eat roast bribard, plus whatever the gods choose to prepare for us." I slid off voolon and helped my mate to the ground, nudging Voolon's flank to urge her to join the herd. "We hunt for meat, and a few select fruits and vegetables, but everything else we eat is gifted to us by the gods."

"I saw the plate ooze from the counter this morning, but I couldn't tell where it came from."

"Let me show you." I extended my hand, holding my breath. Would she brush it aside?

"Yes, show me." With a smile, she linked our fingers together.

We walked to the central dining area, finding almost everyone gone. It was late. Many would have eaten already and returned to their homes. A few sat around the fire blazing in the middle of the open area, and they watched as we passed.

My mate stopped beside Jessia. "We sort of met, but I couldn't communicate with you or tell you how nice it is to meet you. I'm Vanessa."

Van-eesa. Van-essa. Yes, that was it. Vanessa. I repeated the correct pronunciation in my head until it felt natural and smooth.

"You can speak Zuldruxian," Jessia said, looking toward me.

"Today, we traveled to speak with the gods," I said.

"Ah." Jessia nodded wisely. "And what did the gods have to say?"

"That my mate would now understand our language." I wouldn't mention that she might leave me in seven days. That was nearly a lifetime from now. I had plenty of time to show her why she belonged here with me.

Jessia gave Vanessa a tusky grin. "Wonderful.

Perhaps you would like to sit with me sometime and tell me stories of where you come from."

"I'd love to." Vanessa's fingers tightened around mine. "I've seen a ton of movies and read many books. I'm not sure where to start. What sort of stories do you want to hear?"

"Stories?" Brulon raced over to join us, his younger brother, Trevar, scrambling behind. "You're going to tell stories?"

"Soon, my youngling." Jessia patted his back. "Our traedor's new mate said she'll share tales from her home with us soon."

The boys looked up at Vanessa in amazement.

"I think I know exactly what story to tell first." Vanessa turned her gaze toward me. The happy look remained in her eyes. Would it stay with her through the next seven days?

"Not now, younglings," I said. "Vanessa is hungry, as am I. We need to eat."

"I promise I'll tell you some stories soon," Vanessa said, stroking first Nuvar's then Brulon's head.

"That's very nice of you. Come along," their mother said, easing toward the open front doorway. "It's nearly time for bed, younglings. Time to take care of your tusks and snuggle in your bed furs."

"Aw, do we have to go to bed right now?" Brulon asked. "I'm almost grown up. Nearly a warrior like Aizor. Put Trevar to bed and let me stay awake longer? I want to practice with my sword so I can defend our clan." He gouged out with the play sword I'd made for him from wood. When he turns fifteen, he'll be gifted with a crystal sword by the gods.

"Bed," she said firmly, sharing a smile with Vanessa. "You can beat the bushes with your sword tomorrow."

With heavy sighs, the boys left with her.

"Children are the same everywhere," my mate said, watching them leave.

"As are males," I said.

A shadow crossed her face. "Not all males but that's a good thing."

She spoke of her hex and his meanness. If only I could avenge her by lobbing off his head. How could anyone treat this amazing female poorly? She was not only lovely to look upon, but she was kind.

Sorrow shadowed her face, and I wanted to make her feel better again. But sometimes, a person had to allow the emotions to come to the surface. Only then could they be broken up and sorted through, the worst of them tossed aside.

We left Jessia to enjoy the fire and walked into the dining area, finding it empty of Zuldruxians.

"There's a big pan of food sitting on the counter. Did the gods leave that?" The fluffy hairlines above her eyes lifted.

"That's probably bribard prepared by Muzzire. As I said, our gods don't provide meat."

"Vegetarian gods?"

"I don't know that term, but they only gift us with vegetables, fruits, and grains."

"In crystal form."

I chuckled at her pout. "You enjoyed the sweet branch on the island."

"It tasted like candy. Some of this morning's breakfast offerings were like eating rocks."

I stopped by the counter, ignoring the bowls sitting next to the pot of stew. "Watch."

She frowned at the empty counter.

Two plates appeared holding food unlike anything I'd seen before.

"Tacos," Vanessa breathed. "They heard me. Tacos!" She flung her arms up into the air and started shifting her lush behind, twirling around. "Tacos. Tacos! I love you, gods." She shook her hands in the air. "You hear that? Truly, I love you!" Stopping, she grinned up at me, her arms flopping against her sides. "If they really want to make me happy," she lifted her voice to a shout, "they'll also give me coffee."

CHAPTER 23

VANESSA

Ask, and ye shall receive.

When Aizor and I walked into the central building the next morning, the smoky, wonderful smell of coffee greeted me. To say I leaped away from Aizor and raced to the back dining area was an understatement. I pretty much flew over to the counter, rubbing my hands when I took in the blue glass pitcher sitting beside a solitary mug.

"Make that two, honey," I said, watching as a second mug formed from the smooth crystal surface. I was still amazed at how this world worked. The crystal alien told me they had a symbiotic relationship with the Zuldruxians, and I was waiting to see what the Zuldruxians did to fulfill their side of the bargain. But if food of choice was on the menu, this place might not be so bad after all. "You're going to love coffee, babe," I told Aizor.

He grunted. Maybe he didn't like being called babe.

We'd slept in our own fur beds last night. I was

tempted to invite him to join me on my bed, but I wanted to give this a day or two before doing anything like that.

I was going to give this a chance and that may include seeing if his huge cock could actually fit inside me. But I wanted to get to know him a little better first.

All this mate stuff spooked me.

"It's a beverage?" he asked, frowning at the black liquid sloshing in his mug.

"I drink it black, so I guess you do too. We could ask for cream and sugar."

"Cream?"

"It's the liquid baby cows drink from a cow's udder."

His face took on a greenish cast. "No cream."

"You're right. It's best black." Turning, I took my mug over to an empty table and he followed. I sat and closed my eyes, sniffing the brew. "It smells just like coffee." My words came out giddy, but I'd been nursing a massive headache from caffeine withdrawal. If this was crystal alien decaf, I was going to cry.

Riding in stasis must've put withdrawal on hold.

Last night, after we'd feasted on veggie tacos, Aizor was skeptical at first, but then he joined Team Taco. After, we'd placed our plates on the counter. Aizor turned and walked away. I watched as the plates melted into the surface. He told me it had been this way since they moved into their crystal homes, that the plates and food would appear whenever they had need and disappear when they were finished. Many tools and weapons as well. He told me they'd only lived among the gods for a year and were amazed at first but had gotten used to their assistance.

I could get used to this too.

Today, I was going to take an inventory of what the crystal aliens gave and what they didn't. And while I wouldn't push it, but one day soon, I was going to ask for pizza.

"What do you think?" I asked after he took his first sip of coffee.

He grimaced. "You enjoy this."

"Very much." And it tasted exactly the way it should. How had the crystal beings gotten it right? "Are your gods everywhere?"

"Everywhere as in beyond this planet?" He shrugged. "I live my life here and in this moment only. I've never considered what might be happening elsewhere. But if our gods are here, why wouldn't they live and thrive on other planets?"

I remembered people speculating that aliens built the Egyptian pyramids and scoffing. Now, I wondered. But he was right. If I chose to remain here, it wouldn't matter what happened on a planet far from this one.

I drained my mug and looked longingly at the pitcher. Aizor lowered his nearly full cup to the table.

"You don't need to drink it," I said.

"You like it. I want to like it too."

"We're different people. We can share things, but we don't need to adore everything the other does."

He nodded. "You won't be insulted if I don't drink it?"

"Not one bit."

"Wonderful." With a smile, he went up to the counter. He returned with the pitcher and refilled my mug, then went back and requested breakfast, lowering the two plates onto the table.

I stared at my crystal meal and wondered how my body would digest it and if my teeth were up to crunching through it.

I wrangled my way through the meal, glad much of it was softer crystal fruit and something that vaguely tasted like a salted caramel protein bar, and we returned our plates to the counter. Like a little kid, I watched them ooze into the surface, leaving only smooth crystal behind.

We were leaving when I spied the small creature from the day before sneaking along the right wall in the main room.

"Wait here?" I said to Aizor, pointing to the animal. "And don't attack it."

"It's a pest," he said, but he patted my shoulder. "I won't kill it. Yet."

I hurried to the counter. "Pet food, please." Feeling a bit like Captain Picard, I watched as a plate with crystal food appeared on the surface. It looked exactly like what I'd eaten for breakfast and my belly had so far accepted. But since the creatures on this planet appeared to be at least part crystal—except for the Zuldruxians—maybe the small beast adored glassy food.

I took the plate into the big room, finding Jessia and four male warriors bristling with crystal swords and spears gathered around Aizor. All of them stared at the creature.

"What is it?" I asked when I joined them. "As in, what do you call that small beast?"

"It's a chall," Jessia said, her lips pursing. "A pest. It sneaks into the dining area and steals food off our plates."

"If you fed it, it wouldn't need to steal food."

Her head tilted, and I could tell she was intrigued, not horrified by the suggestion. "Interesting idea. Why would we feed it?"

"Other than to keep it away from your meal? Because it would reward you."

"I don't see how a chall could reward me with anything."

"It reminds me of little creatures we have on my home planet called a cat. It's fluffy like them and it looks soft in a glassy way." Would its spiky fur lie down if and when I patted it? Who was I kidding? It was a wild, feral creature. It wasn't going to let me near it. "If I can tame it, it would be my friend."

"We're friends with each other." Jessia continued to frown. "Though I can see the benefit of keeping it away from our meals."

"Come on, little chall," I cooed, tiptoeing toward it with the plate extended.

Its gaze trained on the crystal yummies, it lifted its nose and sniffed.

When I got within five feet of it, I stopped and placed the plate on the floor.

"You're feeding it?" Aizor sounded completely puzzled. "I don't understand."

"This is a way to show it I don't mean it harm. Back on Earth, I volunteered at an animal rescue. It was common for us to take in feral creatures like this. We made sure they were healthy, neutered them, then released them back where they came from."

"Neutered?"

"Cut off male balls."

His face blanched. "Please tell me you don't intend to do anything like that here."

I shot him a grin. "Behave and your balls are safe from me." I lifted my fingers and made a snipping gesture like I held scissors. "Misbehave and you'll need to sleep with one eye open." Not really. He was too adorable and too sexy to contemplate something like that, but it never hurt to keep a guy on his toes.

The other guys slipped away from us and with wide eyes, hurried toward the kitchen.

I turned back to watch the chall creeping closer to the plate. It kept a sharp eye on me and the others, though it must be used to seeing Zuldruxians around all the time if it regularly snuck into the building to steal food. When it reached the plate, it started gulping it down, chomping through the crystalline chunks with its thick jawline and needle-sharp teeth.

Stooping down, I extended my hand toward it.

Aizor hissed but remained with Jessia. The chall shot him a growl but only studied my hand while tilting its head to chew through a long piece of food with the side of its mouth.

I eased closer.

It scowled but food won out and it kept eating.

When I was near enough to touch, I gently ran my fingertips across the top of its head and down its spine. Its crystal fur was surprisingly soft, and I created static with the rub.

Its tail whipped back and forth, and it eyed me while gnawing through its growl.

"Take care, mate," Aizor said. "I wouldn't want it to bite you."

I could only imagine how painful that might be, but I kept stroking.

The chall finished the meal but remained where it was, cocking its head to watch my hand stroke its spine.

"What should we call you, little one?" I asked.

"No one names challs." Aizor's hand landed on my shoulder, and he squeezed. "Please be careful."

"I will. I've done this before. Many times."

Because I didn't want to push it, I eased backward and stood, watching as the chall licked the plate. It looked up at me in thanks before it spun on its hind legs and bolted from the building.

Shaking her head and smiling, Jessia strolled toward the front door.

"First step accomplished," I said. "Actually, I'm surprised it tolerated me touching it. What do you think about calling him Franklin?"

"Franklin?"

"That's the name of my old boss."

"We don't name challs."

"I do." After returning the plate to the kitchen, I linked my arm through Aizor's and tugged him toward the door. "What's on the agenda for today?"

He shot me a tusky grin that made my insides do a little dance. "Besides seducing my pretty mate?"

"Where would you do something like that?" I was truly curious how far he'd take this. It was clear he'd seen my seven-day ultimatum as a challenge, and from the heat coiling from my belly to between my legs, my body was quite eager to see what plans he had to convince me to stay.

"After I speak with my second, Krute, I believe we should bathe in the pools."

Warm water. Sitting inside a pool with Aizor?

Sign me up.

AIZOR

I had six days left, and I wasn't going to waste any of them. I would win Vanessa's heart, and she'd tell me she wanted to stay.

With a plan in mind, I sought out Krute to get our talk over with, though we didn't have much to discuss. His scouts had spied a herd of bribards in the small valley adjacent to the one with the island housing our gods, and he thought we should put together a hunting party to take down three to cure. We stored dried, smoked meat for the cool, winter months, and with fall approaching and the nights getting chilly, now was an excellent time to do it.

"Anything else?" I asked him. We sat at the central firepit in the middle of our ring of homes, though the fire wasn't lit.

"Muzzire swears he found footprints in the woods above our village."

"Nevarn's clan?" I asked sharply.

Vanessa, who was studying the wooden chair I made Jessia, even sitting in it and rocking with a big smile on her face, paused to look our way.

Krute shrugged. "He said the footprints were big. Much bigger than any Zuldruxian he's seen before. I suppose they could be from the Celedar Clan."

"Our males chased them away a few days ago. What reason would Nevarn, or his males, have to keep coming this far from their forest home?"

We both looked at Vanessa.

A growl rumbled in my chest. I'd slice Nevarn through, sew him back together, then slice him all over again if he so much as touched my mate.

"Post more guards," I said.

Krute nodded, and we both stood. "I'll do so right away."

"Also send two males to look for a woman like Vanessa."

Her smile widened, and I loved seeing the thanks in her eyes.

Krute's thick brow ridge tightened. "A female?"

"Yes." I explained about the women inside pods on the island and how Vanessa noted one of them was missing. "If they find her, bring her to us. We'll keep her safe."

"I will." He started to leave but turned back. "About *your* god-given mate."

I cocked my head.

Coming back to stand beside me, he lowered his voice. "She wants to leave, doesn't she?"

Not if I had anything to say in it. "Not yet."

"You should send her back. I still . . ." He growled.

"You still believe we shouldn't respect the gifts from the gods?"

"They don't belong here. None of them." With a snarl, he left to seek out the other males.

Grumbling, I walked over to stand in front of Vanessa.

"Is everything alright?" she asked.

"Everything will work out as it should." I shot a glare at Krute's spine.

She rubbed her fingertips along the intricately carved armrest. "This is a gorgeous piece of work."

"I made it," I croaked, proud that she admired it so much.

"You did? It's beautiful. You're quite talented."

"Thank you. Are you ready to bathe now?"

Her gaze narrowed on my face. "Yes." Hesitancy came through in her voice, but I wouldn't do anything with my mate she wouldn't enjoy.

I held out my hand. "Walk with me, and I'll select the perfect pool. Warm but not too hot."

And completely isolated from the rest. For a female who let me lick between her legs while she was braced against the wall inside the central meeting building housing my gods, my mate was surprisingly shy about revealing her body to others.

"Do we need to get clothing?" she asked, pinching the tunic she wore. "This one needs a good wash." She squinted around as we walked up the hill to the cave entrance. "You said there's no laundromat? I assume I'll need to take my turn at the local river with a rough rock."

"What's a lawndamatt?"

She explained.

I still didn't understand. "The gods wash our clothing, though wash is an odd way to put it."

"I'm trying to picture crystal gods kneeling on a riverbank, scrubbing tunics in the water with soap made from . . . lye." She frowned. "I think that was how they made soap long ago on Earth."

"I've told you our gods only reside within the crystal structures."

"Can they move? Like, uproot a structure and take a stroll through the valley?"

"Our gods are as immovable as the trees. They dwell within the spires that long ago sent roots deep below the ground. When a disease swept across this world, many of us died and most of the crystal gods went dormant. Only a few care enough to interact with us now."

"Like the ones on the island."

"Those and one here within my clan. Only a few gods remained for each clan while the rest . . . I assume they're gone forever. It's been a very long time." I grunted. "As for washing, the gods absorb our soiled clothing and return it or something similar to it while we bathe."

"Absorb like the plates?"

"Yes. I mentioned their roots sink deeply. They network everywhere below the ground."

"I didn't see any in the mountain caverns."

"They are there, below the stone."

"I see."

"Isn't this how you obtain food and clean clothing where you come from? Why kneel at a riverbank or lean over the fire to sear meat? I cannot imagine such a thing."

"We don't have gods like yours."

This couldn't be true. "Who performs these tasks for you, then?"

"We do it ourselves." She lifted her arm and clenched her fist, massaging the muscle in her upper arm. "Exercise keeps us healthy."

"Ah." I nodded, still not exactly sure what she meant.

"Didn't you have to do all this for yourself not long ago? You said you only recently moved into your crystal homes."

"Some things were still done for us by the gods, though we tried to ignore that fact."

"Why?"

"Because we thought they'd harmed us."

"I see. Do your gods also vacuum?" she asked, gazing around raptly. I liked that she was enjoying her time on Zuldrux. "And what do you do about disposable goods?"

"I don't understand your words."

We reached the entrance to the cave and walked inside, pausing to allow the lectums to bloom on the ceiling above us.

"A vacuum is something we use to clean."

"The gods keep everything tidy as well."

"Amazing," she breathed. "That's . . . No cleaning? It's like heaven. As for disposable goods, I'm referring to things like bags to store stuff in, paper cups you throw out. Trash, I guess. It's disposable, meaning disposed of when it's no longer needed."

"We use everything and whatever we don't need is absorbed into the ground by the gods. There's no need to throw things. We're gentle when we lay them on the ground or on the counter."

"What do the gods get in exchange for serving you?"

"We honor them."

"I have to say, this beats burning disposable goods or covering them with dirt in a landfill. I . . ." Her smile rose. "I like it. Your gods are the kings and queens of recycling."

"Our gods are not male or female."

"Do they procreate at all?"

"As far as I know, they don't have sex."

"How do they make baby gods?"

I snorted. "There's no such thing. They're here. Their crystal structures cover our world. And their network of roots thrives below the ground, serving our needs while we worship them."

"That's it? They do everything for you in exchange for being thanked?"

"What else would we give them?" I asked, puzzled by her amazement.

"Blood?"

I lifted my brow ridge. "What would they do with our blood?"

"It's a long story. When you're up for a scary tale, I'll share it."

She said so many confusing things, yet I found her exciting to speak with. I wanted to hear all about her world and talk to her about mine.

"You thank your gods and that makes them happy," she said with a sigh. "How can you tell this makes them feel good?"

"They glow."

Her breath caught. "I don't believe I've seen that."

"You did last night."

"You mean . . . That's right. I thought it was something like the northern lights." She explained what she meant.

"I believe, my pretty mate, you will see these lights again tonight."

"I can't wait."

I had six days left, and she was eager to experience things in my world.

It was a start.

CHAPTER 25
VANESSA

We bathed and returned to our home, finding the bedding tidied, Aizor's loincloth he'd tossed on the floor last night . . . absorbed. And snacks waiting on a crystal plate.

"I believe your people are the true gods here, not the other way around."

His bright laughter rang out.

I slumped on the bed furs, gaping up at him. Damn, he was gorgeous when he laughed. Why hadn't I seen how handsome he was right from the start? The attacking creature may have distracted me, but Aizor . . .

I'd thought him beastly, and I supposed he was in an alien sort of way. But he was my beast, a very sexy one. I was glad I could see it now. I wasn't ready to make my decision—it hadn't been enough time—but boy, it would be tough to leave Zuldrux. No, it would be torturous to leave Aizor.

"We're not the gods here," he said, still chuckling.

"They cater to your every wish."

"Not all. We ask, and many times, we don't receive what we wish for."

"Why not?"

"They decide."

"Okay." Could I learn what the crystal aliens provided and what they didn't and find a way to fill the gap? Not with disposable items. Who needed trash lying around in this pristine world? But . . . "If I stay, I can't sit around doing nothing."

"I don't know what you mean." He joined me on the furs, placing the bowl between us. He picked up and ate a pink crystal ball the size of a large marble, crunching through it. He laid other bowls holding small, odd crystal objects in various colors near the first bowl.

I lifted and licked one, finding it tasted vaguely like a grape. When in Rome . . . I popped it into my mouth and ground it with my teeth, enjoying the burst of flavors enough to grab a thin blue thing half the length of a pencil and about as thick. "I had a job back on Earth. I was a cook. You don't need a cook here, not when your gods will craft any dish you ask for." My shoulders slumped.

"We do prepare our meat dishes, but that's Muzzire's favorite task."

"He's the grumpy one, right?"

He nodded.

"I wouldn't want to encroach on his territory, but I love to prepare meals for people," I said. "I was studying to be a chef. I had this big old dream about one day owning my own restaurant, of crafting exquisite dishes my customers would rave about."

"Much like our gods, you also enjoy praise."

"Who wouldn't?"

"You're beautiful."

My laugh snorted out. "Thanks, but that's not exactly what I meant." I bit the end off the blue pencil, finding it tasted like strawberries. This must be the gods' version of a fruit platter. So far, my intestines hadn't protested what I'd eaten. Maybe I *could* survive on crystal food like the Zuldruxians.

"Tell me what you mean, then," he said. "I'll help you all I can. I want you to be happy here." He tilted my face and kissed me, the flavors from the fruit making him taste even sweeter.

"I'm going to see exactly what can be produced in the kitchen, and then think about it," I said after he leaned back and gave me a sweet smile.

"What else could you do that would give you pleasure?"

I could think of a lot of things I'd like to do with Aizor that would give me pleasure, but I didn't think he meant sexy stuff.

"You work with wood sometimes," I said. "That chair . . . you could sell objects like that at craft fairs. Which you don't have. Or need, I guess."

"Yes, I cut the trees and mold wood from them. I enjoy building things." He shrugged, his cheeks darkening and his gaze darting away from mine. "It's a simple thing, but it makes me happy."

"Could you show me your shop? I have a few ideas for other things I could do here."

"Of course. Tell me what you want, my pretty mate, and it's yours."

This guy was making me reconsider everything I'd always thought I needed back on Earth.

And I wasn't exactly sure what I should do about it.

Abstinence seemed to have become Aizor's new best friend. There had been no repeat of the amazing oral and finger sex he'd given me, and while I woke each morning to him lying beside me with a rip-roaring hard-on that had to be uncomfortable, he'd only smile, kiss me sweetly, and slip from the furs.

We shared a bed, lots of conversation while strolling along the paths meandering through the woods near his crystal village, and mealtimes, but no sex.

With four days left until I had to give the crystal aliens my decision, I still wasn't sure what I wanted to do.

While I could easily imagine myself living here forever, I should want to return to where I came from, right?

"Rise, my pretty mate," he said, leaning over the bed I still lounged in to tap my ass. He tugged the fur blanket down and the heat of his gaze made my skin tingle.

I'd taken to wearing a thin tunic to bed each night and the crystal aliens, somehow knowing this, made sure a clean one lay at the foot of my fur-covered bed each evening. If I thought too hard about it, I'd find it creepy. Instead, I'd started to shrug it off, as if we had people working here who weren't keen on showing themselves to us. As long as they didn't hang around watching us through crystal eyes, I was good.

"I'm sleepy," I said. "Let me lounge in the furs. I need a phone to scroll the internet until I wake up fully. A head-sized cup of coffee. A spinach smoothie because crystals aren't cutting it for greens."

He dropped down to crawl all over me. Yum. He made a fine substitution for anything I might be craving.

First, he started kissing my shoulder. I playfully swatted him away, but when his mouth moved to my neck, I moaned and gave in—like I had when he first touched me. I'd suspected he was holding himself back, and I couldn't blame him. Why invest time and sexual favors in someone who might leave you?

The more he held himself back, however, the more I wanted him. If he was a guy back on Earth, I'd suspect he did it on purpose. This was Aizor, however, a cinnamon roll alien with a gorgeous body, a tongue that should be patented, and the sunniest personality I'd ever found in a man.

I craved him much more than I should.

A few twists and tugs, and my night tunic went flying, fluttering onto the floor. Aizor devoured my breasts, sucking on one nipple then the other, making them form hard nubs that throbbed. My core joined in on the act, catching fire, and I was soon so far gone, I forgot about everything but him.

I knew right then and there that I'd never meet anyone who'd match this guy in the furs. Or outside the furs, now that I thought about it. But who could think when he was kissing down across my belly, murmuring about how pretty I was, how he adored my lush shape, how he was famished and only eating me would give him complete satisfaction?

When he kissed the top of my pussy, I spread my legs and welcomed him home.

He shot me a tusky smile and nudged my thighs wider.

"Mine," he growled, his head diving between my legs. He ran his nose through my saturated folds, still snarling. "Mine. All mine. Mine, mine, mine." He sucked in a breath and exhaled a groan before his tongue stabbed out, driving inside my passage.

"Fuck," I bellowed.

"*Fook*," he mumbled in reply. "*Fook eff.*"

His fingers stroked through my folds, making me drip with anticipation. While he kept gliding his tongue inside me, he slid his fingertips up to my clit.

I barked a cry and bucked up to meet him, nearly dislodging his tongue. That would be a true shame. He braced my body with one arm while the other tended to my clit, rolling and teasing it until it throbbed with need.

"You," he snarled before pushing his tongue deep within me once more. "Taste," Another thrust, "Incredible. I tried to . . . hold myself . . . back, but I . . . can't any longer."

Hunger throbbed within me, an aching need only Aizor could fill. Completely lost and crying out loud enough to wake dormant crystal gods, I jerked my hips up to meet his mouth. I rode his face while he growled, nibbled, and licked, his tongue deep within me before sliding out to drag across my clit.

His fingers joined the party, thrusting inside me along with his tongue.

Whimpering, I clung to the furs before latching onto his hair, holding him close to my core.

When I came, he twisted his tongue inside me, driving me even higher. I crashed in heavy waves, my body shuddering. He kept moving his fingers inside me, alternating with his tongue, until my body was so sensitive, I couldn't stand it.

Then he rocked back onto his heels and licked his face clean. "Rest, my pretty mate, because now that breakfast is finished, I believe I'll devour my lunch."

CHAPTER 26

AIZOR

There wasn't anything I wouldn't do to sink my cock deep within Vanessa. But I was waiting for her to give me a sign that this was what she wanted more than anything. It would be wrong to just . . . do it until she told me it was what she needed.

With only two days left, I didn't know what else I could do to convince her she belonged by my side. I'd talked with her, teased out her smiles, taken walks with her, and even helped her feed Franklin.

I hadn't given up. Soon, I'd show her my surprise. That might make all the difference.

I kept dreaming . . .

She'd tell me she wanted everything. I'd spoken with Muzzire and he'd reluctantly agreed she could prepare one meal per week. Once I told her, she'd say she'd be quite happy working with the god beneath our dining area. She'd *expereemunt* with her *ressapees*. No, those weren't the right words, but I couldn't remember exactly what they were.

If she felt complete here, she'd never want to leave.

After I'd made sure she came three times, we left our home, heading toward the dining area.

Franklin slunk along the edge of the woods, watching her.

"See?" She pointed to him. "He likes me."

"He likes what you feed him."

"He's letting me touch him all the time, now," she breathed. "You saw that yourself. One of these days, he'll climb onto my lap."

"And bite you."

"Nah, not Franklin. This isn't all about food. He craves affection as much as anyone else."

As much as me?

"I'm going to keep working with him." She glanced up at me, frowning. "No one will mind, will they?"

"Why would they?"

"You don't have pets here."

"We have our hepadons."

"I'm not sure it's the same thing, though it's similar. You use your hepadons for riding. You don't snuggle with them."

"I stroke Voolon's snout."

She laughed. "And she loves it when you do it."

"As do you."

Her laughter grew louder. "You're right. I do."

I swallowed hard, trying not to get too hopeful, but

she loved something I did for her? I'd stroke her snout all day long if she'd gift me with one of her smiles.

I tilted my head, waving for her to enter the dining area ahead of me. "How can this be different? I still can't imagine why you want to touch a chall."

"He's cute. Fluffy in a crystal way."

"So is Voolon."

"It's different." She shook her head as we walked through the open room to what she called the kitchen. "You don't bring Voolon into your home."

"She's huge. Why would I do that?"

"Franklin's little. Can't you picture him sleeping in the furs with us? Snuggling when it gets cold?"

"No."

"You're looking at me like I'm out of my mind." Her laugh burst out again. "You might enjoy having him in bed with us."

"Would he watch when I suck on your clit?"

"Oh," she gasped. "I don't think so. I hope not! But don't think I didn't see you extending your finger to him yesterday. He sniffed it."

"His whiskers tickle. I like that."

"You wanted to touch him. Admit it."

I shrugged. "Perhaps a little. He's intriguing. Useless, but intriguing."

"Just because you can't ride or eat him, it doesn't mean he's useless. Small pets can provide great comfort. You stroke them, they purr, and you feel happier."

"If he makes you happy, I guess he could come inside our home. But he is not allowed on our furs."

Her smile only grew. "You'll see."

I wasn't sure about that.

We entered the kitchen and walked up to the counter. Since it was early in the day, no one had made stew—something Vanessa could do if cooking pleased her. Muzzire didn't seem interested in preparing morning or midday meals.

When we stopped at the counter, two plates emerged before we could make our request.

"Food's up," Vanessa quipped as she had each time a plate appeared. "I still can't get over this. It's . . . magical."

Special enough to make her want to stay? The closer it got to the deadline, the more worried I became. What would I do if she told me she was leaving?

I . . . loved her. A big mistake on my part, but I couldn't help it. No, I wouldn't stress. I had a few days left. Surely that was enough time to convince her she belonged here with me.

Vanessa poked the stack of flat, circular things on her plate.

"I don't believe I've ever seen anything like this before." Skeptical, I stared at my plate but didn't touch the food. "What's the brown liquid pooling around the flat circles?"

She dipped her finger into it and popped it into her mouth. When her eyes lit up and she wiggled, moaning, my cock stirred. I swore I was erect whenever I was around my mate. My balls ached almost as much as my heart.

"It's syrup. And these are *pancakes*," she breathed, lifting her arm and hooting while dancing in a circle, nearly sending her food onto the floor.

I enjoyed the sway of her lush ass, wishing we were alone so I could touch it. I'd also like to lift her onto a table, toss up her tunic, and dine on *her* again instead of these cakes on a pan, a name that made no sense since they lay on a plate.

"What is that?" Jessia asked, peering at my dish.

"Pancakes and syrup," Vanessa announced, hugging her plate. "Let's chow, Aizor." She spun and strutted over to a table.

I stared at her ass.

"Your feelings for her have grown," Jessia observed.

"*Fook eff.*"

"*Fook* what?" she asked, her face twisting.

"*Fook eff* is . . ." How to best describe this? "A word Vanessa uses to express joy. She makes me happy."

"I see that." Jessia nodded sagely. "I'll keep these words close and use them at the appropriate moment. I cannot, however, find *fook eff* in the gods' offering this morning. I hope my plate does not contain flat circles with brown liquid oozing around them."

Her breakfast lifted through the counter, and she sighed with happiness, taking it. "Moobars and troolon. Perfect." She turned and hefted it. "*Fook. Fook eff!* I can't wait to eat."

Vanessa stared at Jessia, her jaw unhinging before she started snickering.

Seeing her happy—the only goal in my life—I

shouted *fook eff*, and it was echoed by everyone in the room.

Wetness poured from Vanessa's eyes, but since she told me this was often an expression of joy, I could only grin as I joined her.

After eating, me only picking at the cakes from the plate with brown liquid because they tasted odd, we left to bathe.

I collected clean clothing for us before I led her down a tunnel to a more isolated pool.

Vanessa walked happily beside me. She swept her hand out toward the walls and the roof of the passage. "I suppose the gods created all this, too."

"If you mean they gave us light, then yes."

"Are you *sure* you're not the gods and them the servants? They cook your food. They—"

"We hunt bribards."

"Okay, you hunt for meat, but they give you almost all of your other food."

"Yes."

"I'm not complaining after breakfast. I'm almost excited to see what they serve for my next meal."

Would food make her want to stay? I kept hoping it would be me.

"They wash and dry and fold your clothing," she added.

I frowned as we started walking down the slope. "I don't believe they fold anything. We leave the bath, and the clothing is waiting. It's draped. Not . . . folded."

"Semantics. They generate lights when you need them. They keep your homes clean."

"We live within their dead structures."

She stopped. "You mentioned that, how you didn't live here until a short time ago, after you and other traedors spoke to the crystal gods."

"Prior to that, my clan lived higher in the mountain. Our homes were crafted from bribard hides."

"Why leave the only home you'd ever known?"

"The gods invited us to live inside their exoskeletons once more. Should we leave them empty? Our ancestors lived within their bones, I suppose you could call them."

"I guess it didn't sink into me that we were sleeping and eating inside their corpses."

"I suppose we are. We don't think of it that way. Our ancestors lived within their structures, and now we do once more. They keep us warm in the winter and cool in the summer. Their exoskeletons are much nicer than our old hide homes. Everyone agrees."

"I still find all of this amazing."

I grinned. "I'm glad you think so." One more reason for her to stay?

"What about jewelry?"

"If you wish for precious stones to wear about your neck or in your ears, I'll collect them for you."

"Where? In your precious stone treasure trove?"

I sensed confusion in her words. I also sensed her tension was rising, though I couldn't imagine why she was unhappy to hear about all the wonderful things the gods would do for her when she agreed to remain here as my mate. "I can show you after we bathe."

"No laptops or cell phones. No Wi-Fi, though I don't imagine there's much I'd Google at this point other than Zuldruxians, which I'm sure will bring up nothing."

We reached the end of the tunnel and paused with the vast network of pools spread out in front of us.

"Your gods even gift you with mates." She was definitely beginning to sound surly.

I savored the sound, actually, because it made fire blaze in her eyes and her heady musk of arousal fill the air. Did she realize she liked me more when she tried to squabble?

"So far, I'm the only one gifted with a mate who I'm greatly devoted to." I added the last, hoping to sooth her.

"The only gifted mate *so far*."

The female with red hair had not been found. My males had returned yesterday and shrugged. Had she been gifted to another Zuldruxian? "You're special. The first for my clan."

"That's not reassuring."

I led her to the right and through another tunnel, continuing until we left the sound of clan chatter behind. The cave system was a network of tunnels containing many small alcoves with private pools. I was taking Vanessa to one I'd enjoyed many times when I wished to be alone. Prior to today, we'd bathed in those behind walls of flowering vines or crystal spikes.

"The other women from Earth are mates-in-waiting," she said. "They're prisoners, held in suspension until your gods decide it's Christmas time and they need to be stuffed inside someone's stocking."

"What's a stocking?"

"That's not the point."

I stopped and lifted her, pressing her against the smooth stone wall. Her legs naturally went around my waist and her hands latching onto my shoulders, both encouraging signs.

"I'm going to kiss you, my pretty mate," I said, staring at her mouth I couldn't wait to consume.

"Why?"

"Because I need you." I said it simply. Could she hear the sincerity in my voice? "You're not mad at *me*."

Her lips pursed. "Maybe I am."

"You're mad at our gods."

"Definitely that." Her body softened. "I'm sorry. I see what you're saying. I'm irritated with their high-handed ways, and I'm taking it out on you. I don't mean to. This . . . is a big adjustment for me."

"Which is why I brought you here today, to a place where we could be alone."

She wiggled the fluff lines above her eyes. "I thought you brought me here so you could take advantage of my willing body."

"Is your body willing?"

Her lips curled up on one side, and her gorgeous eyes glowed. "It could be persuaded."

"What about your mind?"

"Don't push it. I'm a work in progress."

Good enough. I tossed her over my shoulder, and

while she laughed and squealed, I carried her inside the alcove holding my favorite pool. No one would disturb us. We would be alone for hours.

Oh, I was going to push it. No doubt about that.

No more waiting.

I was going to push it deep inside her.

CHAPTER 27
VANESSA

I was very much in like with Aizor. Waking with his woody pressed against my spine and his heavy breathing in my ear made me feel all dreamy. It made me wonder what it would be like to stay here with him forever.

I wasn't a woman who needed a man to tease her body to the point she lost control and let him have fun. No dub-con for me. I liked sex if it was with the right guy. I had a feeling sex would be amazing with Aizor.

Yes, I was playing with fire with my favorite caveman. Although, calling him a caveman wasn't exactly true. While his clan used caves for bathing and maybe the imaginary treasure trove I'd mentioned, they lived in crystal structures that rivaled architectural wonders back on Earth.

They dressed like ancient Romans half of the time, for heaven's sake. And they were catered to by beings they called gods.

Did I want to return home? Funny how thinking the word didn't make longing churn through me. If anything, my heart ached when I thought about leaving Aizor.

He carried me inside a round cave about twenty feet across and with a ceiling two stories high. A steaming pool dominated the room.

"Do your gods spy on you all the time?" I asked when he placed me on my feet and teased at the knot holding my gold belt in place at my waist. To make this easy for him, I untied it and tossed it aside. It remained on the floor.

"They don't spy," he said.

"They must be watching, or they wouldn't know it was time to make food or take your clothing to the big laundromat in the sky."

"They . . ." He huffed but grinned. "You're teasing me."

I poked his bare chest. "No, you're a tease." He'd gone tunic-less today, and I'd been admiring the view. His loincloth barely covered the center of his butt cheeks, leaving all those droolworthy muscles exposed. Just like when we were walking to the kitchen earlier, I kept slinking back to walk behind him until he caught on, scooped me up, and spun me around, ending his laughing tease with a heady kiss that only made me crave him more.

Maybe I was a little bit, a teensy bit, a whole lot more than in like with Aizor.

He ran his fingertips along the low bodice of my

tunic, his knuckles grazing the tops of my breasts. "I adore teasing you. Kissing you. And . . ." His eyes lit up. "I haven't massaged your feet yet. I promised this not long after you arrived, and I haven't done so."

"That's been a sore spot between us. A true dereliction of duty on your part, *mate*."

"I love it when you call me mate, Vanessa," he growled.

He swept my tunic up and over my head, tossing it to the floor near my belt. "As for your question." His gaze was locked on my breasts. Since he'd shredded my underwear back at the island, I didn't have anything other than god-provided clothing to wear. They seemed to believe going commando was a thing. "The gods don't travel this deep within the cave system."

"You mean we'll have to take care of our clothing ourselves? We'll have to wear the same things after we bathe?" I tried to sound scandalized, but he was too cute for anything like that, and my stern look dissolved into smiles and laughter.

"I took the liberty of bringing drying cloths and new clothing down earlier." He tilted his head to outfits draped—not *folded*—and lying on a boulder nearby.

"Well, aren't you handy?" I slid my fingertip beneath the tie of his loincloth.

"I am very handy." He lifted his hands, displaying them to me.

"Where do you plan to place those hands?" My skin was buzzing with electricity, and if we kept teasing each other like this, I was going to combust. Burn the entire place down. Figuratively speaking. This was a stone cave, after all.

"Wherever you'll let me place them." He said this in a sweet, husky way, and his eyes glowed with desire.

I couldn't resist.

"Why don't you show me everything you have to offer, Aizor." I leaped into his arms, and he latched onto me, pulling my body flush against his.

He held me while wrenching his loincloth off, chucking it over his shoulder. Then he climbed into the pool and settled on a natural stone seat. Truly, Zuldrux was amazing. Hot spring pools. Hot alien guys like Aizor. And any food at my command.

The only thing missing was tampons.

I was going to mention that later.

I straddled his waist with his big ole cock thrusting between us. Without any effort on his part, his heat seeking missile, aka, his second cock, glided around the big one and latched onto my exposed clit.

"*Fuck*," I groaned.

"At your command, my pretty mate."

"I meant, holy Batman, fuck." My eyeballs rolled back in my head, and I thrust my body close to his while his second cock did its duty.

Forget hot springs and tampons. I could totally get used to this.

"*Fook eff*," he said with a nod.

Ha. I was going to have to explain a few things —later.

He tilted my chin and his mouth claimed mine. I was

soon lost in the pleasure of his lips and the way his tongue thrust inside. I clung to his shoulders and rocked against him while his small cock continued to give my clit the attention it needed.

His fingers slid down to my breasts, and he rolled my nipples. I was going to come before we got started, and that would be a complete shame.

His physical attributes couldn't be denied, but I wanted this guy for other reasons. He epitomized kindness, and I'd seen how he adored the few children in his clan. He'd built a chair for Jessia where she could rest her bones in the evening and still enjoy the fire.

He was everything I could ever ask for in a guy.

Was I ready to say I do?

I'd decide later. There were more intriguing things going on below the surface of this pool.

I stroked his cock. I couldn't stay away. Big, I could just fit my fingers around it. I wasn't faint of heart, but I was daunted at the idea of that stuffing itself inside me. I'd try, though, and we'd see how it went. Aizor wasn't one who'd force this or hurt me, and I was going to trust in that.

"Vanessa," he growled as I rubbed up his shaft and returned to the base to do it all over again. His obvious pleasure in such a simple thing on my part flooded me with desire. Excitement surged through me. I'd never realized how much satisfaction I could get by pleasing someone else.

His second cock continued to tease my clit, and I worried I'd come before we did much more than this. I rocked against him, and it was all I could do to focus on his cock and not just lay back in the water and let his second cock take me all the way to the stars.

We kissed again, his mouth hot and insistent on mine. I was a moaning wreck already, and I wasn't sure I could take much more. But we'd just gotten started.

Once I'd had a full taste of Aizor, would I ever be able to leave him behind?

Don't think about that. Think about now.

I was soon lost in the stroke of his hands on my sides and the feel of his mouth on mine. My need grew while his second cock continued to throb on my clit.

When he ran his thumbs across my breasts, I ripped my mouth away from his only to cry out, the hoarse sound echoing in the cave.

I tightened my legs around him, pumping against him, so far gone I'd never pull myself out.

Heat roared through me, feeding my need for everything. My skin was on fire.

Water sloshed around us as we moved together, my hands gliding along his cock, his groans barreling up his throat. Mews of need erupted from me as my body got ready to blast off into outer space.

Unable to take much more, I backed away, sliding off his lap. I tried to stand but my legs wouldn't support me, so I latched onto his arms, holding tight.

"No, mate?" he asked and while I could hear disappointment in his voice, I also heard acceptance. If I said I couldn't do this, he'd back off. *This* was why I was falling for this guy. He wanted me more than anything, but he wouldn't push me. I suspected he'd wait for me forever, and that made my heart pinch tight.

"Yes," I said. "Very much yes. But . . . I feel like I'm about to explode, and I want more before that happens."

"Ah." He nodded wisely, his lips curling up on one side. "I can give you more."

Hell, yeah, he could.

"I'm going to climb back on your lap, and I'm going to ride that amazing cock. Try to, that is."

"And my second cock will return to your glorious clit."

No one had ever called my clit—or anything about me—glorious before, and for a heartbeat, I let that sink in.

Then I climbed back on top of him, and he held me with his big hands on my hips. When I lifted myself, he placed the head of his cock at my opening. The water here, like in the pools above, felt silky, as if it contained something that not only moistened the skin but could work well as lube. It seemed I was about to find out.

While I braced myself above him, he stroked the head of his cock across my opening, making sure to nudge my clit with each pass. Who needed his second cock when I had this?

His eyes locked on mine, and he kissed me again, his mouth almost feral, sucking at my lips before he plunged his tongue inside.

I bucked against his cock, needing him deep inside me, too far gone now to care if it would fit.

Lifting, I dropped down onto it at the same time as

he thrust up. Only part of it went inside, and the stretch . . . it stung before the heat simmering inside me blazed, driving me to rise and drop onto him once more. With each descent, he pushed up, slowly sinking his incredible cock deeper.

I was on fire. Nothing was going to put me out other than Aizor. And he knew it. The certainty of it smoldered in his eyes and in the confident way he teased my nipples to ripe buds. He knew exactly how to drive me out of my mind.

When his cock was finally seated all the way inside me, we both groaned. I remained in place for a moment, letting the incredible feeling sink all the way into my bones.

Then I started moving, my gaze locked on his. He watched my face, and I sensed he was waiting for a cue from me about what he should do. But the strain of holding back showed in the creases on his face, the way his arm muscles bunched, and the tight way he gripped my hips with his big fingers.

"Second cock?" he rasped. "Tell me what you need, mate."

"You. This. Everything," I panted.

"It's already yours." He started moving, thrusting up to meet my jerky motion.

And when his second cock latched onto my clit, I pretty much rocketed all the way to the two moons.

Caught up in the amazing feeling, I bucked against him. I clung to his arms and tipped my head back, my eyes closing. So much of this male was wrapped up in the gentle stroke of his fingers on my back and sides and in the way he cupped my breasts before rubbing his thumbs across my nipples.

The water was slippery, making my skin glide across his, his cock slick easily inside me.

Heaven save me from hot pools full of lube.

My keening cries grew louder, mixing in with his groans of need. I was going to burst into flames. They'd consume me and like a phoenix, I'd be reborn from the ashes.

When my orgasm started rippling through me, I succumbed to the heady feeling. To the growing emotions in my heart.

And to Aizor.

My mate was infinitely precious. I'd do anything to make her happy, to make her want to remain with me forever.

So after her lovely body found pleasure in mine, and I released myself inside her with a groan that echoed throughout the caverns, I held her. I stroked her back and told her how amazing she was, how much I adored her.

I lifted her off my body, hers sucking on my cock in a greedy way that made me want to arouse her once more and stake my claim on everything she had to offer. But showing her I could offer her more than good cock was in order.

I placed her on a high seat, still within the pool, and she leaned back on the smooth stone. She mumbled something, and the heady smile on her face as her head tilted back made me want to climb all over her again. Instead, I knelt in front of her, lifted one of her feet, and gently placed it on my thigh.

"Ticklish," she said, her eyes still closed.

I began massaging her foot, using broad strokes up the bottom of her foot and a softer touch on her toes.

"Pink," I said.

"Hmm?"

"Your toenails are bright pink."

"Polish. Gels. I don't suppose your crystal gods could arrange for something like that, could they? Because the gels won't last forever."

Since I didn't even know what *pooleesh* or *jules* were, I shrugged.

I continued massaging her foot before lowering it and doing the same with the second. She groaned through it, and frankly, each hissing sound of pleasure she made shot straight to my main cock, making it stiffen once more.

Finished with her second foot, I began on her legs, savoring how lovely they felt beneath my palms, how tiny she was, and how nicely her gods had made her. Her body was lush in all the right places, such as her plump ass and her belly . . . She truly was a gift from our gods, and I'd thank them every day of my life as long as she remained with me.

"Mmm," she said as I made broad circles on her flesh, the natural balm in the water making her skin slippery.

I kept going, stroking her knees and teasing the backs of them even when it made her breathing hitch with laughter. Her smile only grew as I moved up her thighs.

When she spread them wider, I accepted her invitation and rubbed her inner legs in broad circles, slowly making my way higher. When I ran my thumb up her crease and across her clit, she jerked up her hips and moaned.

She was incredibly responsive, and I was honored that she wanted to give her body to me. Each time she did, I'd make sure she found pleasure, not just take it myself.

I slid a finger inside her, groaning at how soft her inner walls were and how they sucked on the digit. She took two fingers just as easily, and my hands were huge compared to her petite size.

When her lips parted and she panted with each thrust of my fingers, I moved over her. I'd die if I didn't kiss her, if I didn't suck on her nipples so unlike a Zuldruxian's nursing tubes.

What would it be like to watch her feed one of our young? Maybe she didn't want younglings herself. That would be alright. As long as I could look at her pretty face each day and grow old by her side, I'd be the happiest male alive.

She melted off her seat and into my arms, and I caught her.

"Would my pretty mate like another taste of my cock?" I purred into her ear as she ran her palms across my chest.

"Your pretty mate is going to snarl if you don't give her your cock very soon."

My grin widened. "Far be it for me to make my mate snarly."

"Aizor." She bucked against my rigid cock. "Now."

"You're a greedy mate."

"Aizor!"

I spun her around and laid her across the smooth area beyond the pool, presenting her ripe ass to me. When I ran the head of my cock between her legs, she bucked back, whimpering.

I fed my second cock beneath her, guiding it to her clit, grateful it could stretch to reach, because the thought of not taking her from this position made me want to lash out and growl.

And when I slid my cock inside her welcoming sheath, she roared out my name.

CHAPTER 29
VANESSA

Five orgasms in one day were about twenty billion times the number I'd had in the last year. My ex had been into his own pleasure more than mine. Actually, I wasn't sure he'd ever cared about mine, which was one of the many reasons I'd left him.

We eventually dried and dressed in the clean clothing Aizor brought, then walked back up to the surface. Sunlight greeted us, along with some of his clan members who needed one thing or another from him.

Since he was busy, I gave him a smile and a stroke down his arm and walked over to the dining area for a snack. I was curious to see how accommodating the crystal gods might be in their effort to please me. They wanted me to stay, and while I wouldn't take advantage of that, I wasn't above making sure I could enjoy some of the comforts of home.

My request for pizza resulted in something that not only didn't resemble pizza, but it also didn't taste like it either. When I suggested a redo of my gel toenails, I was met with silence.

The crystal countertop did, however, produce some food for my chall friend, Franklin, and I went looking for him, finding him lounging in the sunshine partway down the trail leading away from the village. He gobbled up what I gave him while I stroked his spine, and I was rewarded when he purred.

"You're just a big old sweetie, aren't you?" I crooned.

"I am," Aizor said from behind me.

I spun, nearly toppling over, and he scooped me up in his arms.

"My mate's unsteady," he said.

"You surprised me."

"A good surprise, I hope."

"The best." I couldn't resist kissing him, but when he made it clear with his roaming hands that he wouldn't mind taking this further, I eased away. "Your cock is amazing."

"Very much so," he said with a smirk.

"What you do with your cock is equally amazing."

His smile only grew, along with the smug look in his gorgeous eyes. He had me, and he knew it. "I completely agree."

"But it's big."

"Well noted."

"My body needs a little time to recover after the latest bout in the pools."

"Ah." He nodded sagely. "I have a cure for that, my pretty mate." With that, he took me back to the village and inside his crystal home, where he laid me on the lush furs.

"I'm not sure you understand," I said.

"Oh, I do, my mate." He lifted a container about the size of his hand. "I hold the cure here."

And beneath his loincloth, no doubt.

I decided to see what he considered a cure.

He opened the top and scooped out a walnut-sized lump of creamy goo. Before I could comment on its bright purple color, he'd flipped up my tunic, latched my legs on his shoulders, and began slathering it between my legs. When he slid a few coated fingers inside me, my moan ripped through the room. He looked up, his grin even bigger. Damn sexy alien. No one should look this cute. It was bad for my heart.

"How do you feel now, precious one?" he drawled.

The cream made my skin tingle, and it warmed as he slid his fingers in and out of me. The slight sting that had made walking interesting earlier melted away, replaced by pure lust.

"You're bad," I groaned, thrusting my hips up to meet his fingers. "Very naughty."

"But it's helping, isn't it?" He eased my legs down and removed my tunic. Then he climbed over me, his fingers buried once more inside me. His thumb found my clit while his tongue entangled with mine.

He kissed me and stroked me until my orgasm shot through me. Chock that up for number six in one day.

He held me after, and despite his engorged cock, he didn't press me for more. I throbbed between my legs, but already, his magical cream was performing miracles. The sting had faded, and I no longer felt chafed.

When I woke after napping, I stretched, luxuriating in the heady feel of fur against my naked skin. Every part of me down south felt normal, and I suspected it was solely due to the cream.

I dressed and went outside, finding Jessia sitting in her chair near the unlit fire, two little boys perched on the ground by her feet, staring up at her raptly. When I walked over to join them, she smiled my way.

"You spoke of sharing tales from your people," she said. "I'd love to hear one if you have time."

The boys wiggling around in excitement was all the incentive I needed. I perched my butt on one of the big rocks encircling the firepit and told them about a lion cub named Simba.

My story was a hit. Even Jessia giving me a tusky grin after.

"Will you tell us another?" Trevar asked. I'd worked my way to the ground, and he'd crawled onto my lap while I acted out parts with a grim voice for the villain, plus a higher pitched one for Nala.

"Tonight," I said, easing him aside. "For now, I need to see how I can incorporate my old job into my new life here."

"Job," Jessia asked. "You mean a task like hunting or . ..?"

When crystal gods took care of most of your needs, who needed to work? There wasn't a store where I could buy things even if I had money, something I suspected the Zuldruxians would find as odd a concept as a big box store.

"The pizza the gods offered needs work," I said. "And I've yet to be served bread, biscuits, or a roll."

Her head tilted. "Rolling what?"

"Exactly."

"We sometimes roll down the hill," Trevar chimed in. "It's fun."

"I want to do that with you."

"You do?" he breathed. "You're not a youngling."

"At heart I am. At heart." I grinned. He was incredibly cute. Everything was cute here, even Franklin who was watching from behind me and Aizor's home. Did he think I didn't see him there? "I can't expect your gods to deliver everything I need," I told Jessia.

"Our needs are few." She laughed. "We are well cared for, however."

"Other than . . ." Funny how I hadn't seen any other abominables since I'd arrived, yet one attacked me. I peered toward the woods as if I expected to see one come roaring out of the bushes on cue, but the world around me remained calm and serene. "Are there *any* threats here?"

"Of course." Jessia looked toward the boys, and I assumed she didn't want to get them worked up. "We have guards. They alert us if anything concerning comes near. And more often, they . . . frighten it away."

Kill it? I guess that beat being killed yourself.

"What do you plan on making in the dining area?"

she asked, changing the subject. "We have plenty of dried bribard."

"That wasn't quite what I had in mind. I was a cook where I came from."

"You prepared food. We do this with meat, something the gods don't favor."

"My specialty was sweets, though I didn't have much call to make more than pies and cake back at the diner."

"What is a sweet?" Trevar chimed in to ask.

"Candy. Ice cream. That sort of thing. Like the branches of the trees on your godly island."

"The gods in the dining area haven't given us anything like that," Trevar's brother, Brulon said, getting to his feet.

"Maybe you'd like to help me?" I said, ruffling his hair. "Then you can eat what we make."

Trevar jumped to his feet. "Me too."

"Let's go see what the gods can offer for ingredients."

With the boys trailing behind me like I was the Pied Piper with a perfectly tuned flute, I walked over to the dining building and went inside.

At the counter, I wasn't sure how to handle this. Aizor said the gods didn't spy on us, but they must've heard me lamenting about the loss of pancakes in my life. I hadn't asked them to make them for me.

"Hey, crystal gods," I said as I stood in front of the counter. "I want to make chocolate chip cookies." I knew many recipes by heart, so I listed the ingredients, using the measurements from back on Earth, unsure how this would work out.

Miraculously, an empty bowl appeared first, followed by shortening, sugar, and all the rest of the ingredients, conveniently dispensed by the counter in the proper amounts.

The boys clung to the counter, their eyes widening with the presentation of each item.

"How can I bake these babies once they're ready?" I asked them.

Their eyes only widened, and they shrugged.

"I need an oven."

"I believe I can help with that." Aizor strode across the kitchen, coming up to me and giving me a kiss on the cheek. Truly, he was a sweetie. No wonder I was seriously contemplating staying.

He took my hand and led me outside, the boys still following, chattering about cookies and speculating what they'd look like, let alone how they'd taste. Brulon was skeptical while Trevar was excited about the idea—a boy after my own heart.

We walked down the hillside, leaving the small village and crystal homes behind, taking a trail weaving through a long, scruffy stand of purple trees. The trail emptied out in another meadow with a rectangular block built of stone with mortar.

Aizor led me over to it, a sly grin on his face. "I built this for you." He patted the structure and took me to one side with a hinged crystal plate in the center. He unlatched and opened it, revealing a crude oven. The pile of wood nearby should've given it away. "You'll be able to make your peeza here," he said proudly. "You said it's often cooked with a wood fire, and I started thinking . . . I don't know if you can make anything else here, but I wanted you to feel . . . at home."

The boys nodded, suggesting they'd been in on the surprise.

I burst into tears.

CHAPTER 30
AIZOR

I'd distressed my pretty mate, and I didn't know what to do about it. The younglings took one look at her and shrieked, running up the trail, disappearing into the woods. I suspected they wouldn't stop until they'd reached their mother. They'd tell her my mate had . . . I wasn't sure what had happened, but she was crying.

"Are you sad or happy?" I asked, tentatively touching her arm. "It could be one or the other, and I need to know which."

She latched onto me, pressing her wet face against my chest. "Happy. So happy!"

This was a relief. "I'm sorry." I patted her back. Should I hold her tighter or . . . I wasn't sure what to do.

"Why are you sorry?" Leaning back in my embrace, she looked up at me.

"I've made you produce water from your eyes again."

"No one's ever built an oven for me before." More tears tumbled down her face. Should I take her to the healer? They might be able to fix this or at least tell me how to make this right. She said she felt happiness, but she didn't sound joyful.

"Then they should've."

"You're so nice and handsome, and I shouldn't be sobbing about it."

"It's kay-kay to cry. Emotions have value, no matter what they are."

"Kay-kay?"

"You say this a lot. Kay-kay."

Her face cleared. "Ah, okay."

"I missed the oh."

"You did." A smile bloomed on her face, not only reassuring me but telling me she *was* happy.

"The guys I've been with in the past never listened, and they certainly never did much for me. A bouquet of flowers, maybe, on Valentine's Day, but the last one forgot our anniversary. He only remembered when he caught me putting together my gift for him. I got a gift card from the convenience store on the corner from him, telling me he'd bolted out and bought it when he realized he had nothing."

I didn't understand much of what she was saying but that part didn't matter. What did matter was that she was telling me that the males she'd been with hadn't put her needs above their own—not ever. And that listening and doing things based on what she said was the best way to please her.

Who would've thought making a mate happy could be this simple?

"Thank you for building me an oven," she said, wetness no longer leaking from her eyes. She started to wipe it from her face, but I stilled her hands and did it for her, swiping it away with my thumbs while she stared at me with so much adoration, it humbled me.

In that moment, I knew that I would only be half a male if she left. Yes, I would live, but how could I go on without the rest of my heart?

"I'm glad you like it. Are you . . . okay?"

She nodded and sniffed. "I'm better than okay." Barreling into me, she hugged me.

I held her, silently praying to the crystal gods that I could convince her that she would also be only half of herself without *me*.

"Would you like to help me make cookies?" she asked. "I seem to have lost my helpers."

"I'd love to."

Holding hands, we returned to the dining area. She started pouring odd-appearing items into a bowl, and when she handed me a large spoon, I stirred.

"Why don't you just ask the gods for food like this?" I asked as she poured flour on top of the creamed sookar and tiny-maker—no, *shortening*.

"And miss out on the fun of making the cookies ourselves?"

"You find joy in the art of creating, not only in eating the result?"

"You made Jessia a chair. Why not just ask the gods to create it for you?"

"I don't know if they could," I said, seeing what she meant already.

"If they could, why bother doing it yourself?"

"You're not only pretty but wise, my mate." I nodded slowly. "I understand what you mean. I enjoy not only cutting the wood and creating smooth boards but molding them into the chair Jessia adores. The look on her face when I presented it? Nothing can match that."

"I'd never suggest you stop asking your gods for things you need. I'm thinking about tampons, here, which I'll need soon, but consider how much fun it could be doing things you enjoy with your own hands. I guess it's like a hobby back on Earth. Many people do things solely because it's fun, not because they can't buy it already made. Or in your case, ask the gods for it."

Her observation stunned me. "I've never considered it this way."

"Then my work is done." She looked around at the empty containers surrounding her bowl. "I don't think we forgot anything. Now we need a flat pan to bake these babies on, though some people love eating the dough raw."

"Are you still here in my cooking area?" someone said.

I glanced toward the opening into the main part of the building, finding Muzzire standing there, scowling. "We're making cookies."

"In *my* kitchen?" His glare fell on my mate. "Where will I find space to make the stew for dinner?"

"We're almost done here," she said. "Baking's next, and we'll do that in the oven Aizor built for me."

"Never mind." Muzzire pivoted and stormed from the room.

"Should I go apologize to him?" she asked. "I don't want him to think I'm taking over."

"There's room in this kitchen for more than one cook."

"True." Her smile bloomed anew. "What were we saying about my cookies?"

"That I would like them raw—like you, mate." I scooped my finger into the bowl and popped the glob into my mouth. Flavors unlike anything I'd tasted before exploded on my tongue. "It's amazing," I mumbled around the bite. "Sweet."

Her grin rose, chasing away any sadness from her eyes. "And that's the second-best part about making cookies—eating them."

"Not as tasty as you, mate."

Color flooded her face. She knew exactly what I meant.

"Cookie batter can sit before it needs to be baked." Her voice came out thready, and her fingers twitched at her sides.

Since a flat plate had appeared on the counter at her request for baking, I laid it over the bowl.

Then I took her hand and led her to our home, where I proceeded to place her on our furs, flip up her tunic, and bury my face between her legs.

CHAPTER 31

VANESSA

My cookies were a hit. As we sat around the fire that night, we consumed them all.

"More," Trevar said, licking chocolate off his face.

His mother laughed. "You ate four. No more. In fact, it's time for bed, younglings." Rising, she held out her hands.

"But . . ." Brulon's voice cratered with devastation. "She was going to tell us a story about a meermaid."

"It won't take long," I said. "I can start the tale tonight and finish it tomorrow."

"Are you sure?" she asked. "It would please them—and me—very much, but you crafted something wonderful for us today already. It seems like a lot to ask you to entertain us as well."

"It's not a problem. Gather 'round, younglings." I patted the ground next to where I sat. The boys scampered over, and even baby Willire gaped in my direction. She'd finished nursing—from a tube projecting from beneath one of her mother's four breasts—and now sat gurgling, kicking her feet. She was adorable. I wanted a baby just like her.

My gaze was drawn to Aizor who sat in one of the chairs he'd crafted himself, watching me. Heat flared in his eyes at my attention, and he gave me a smile that made everything inside me melt.

I had to give the crystal alien my decision in two days.

What was it going to be?

To avoid thinking about it, I started the story about the mermaid, and everyone was soon enthralled. Everything was new to these people, and I'd watched a lot of movies and read thousands of books. I had enough stories for three lifetimes.

When the boys started yawning, I smiled at their mom. "And I'll continue this story tomorrow."

"Aw, what about the prince?" Brulon asked. "And how can the mermaid make him love her if she can't talk?"

My gaze was drawn to Aizor. "I believe the prince will find a way."

"Aww, please?" Burlon asked.

"You'll have to wait until tomorrow night to find out what happens next. I promise you're going to be happy with the ending." Here, no one knew what a happily ever after was, but they'd soon learn.

The boys left and not long after that, so did most of the Zuldruxians, heading to bed now that it was dark.

Aizor and I put out the fire and went to his home. Our home?

I'd decided I was going to tell him my decision tomorrow. I didn't want to wait to tell the crystal aliens first. Aizor deserved to be the first to know.

"Should we bathe before going to bed?" I asked him.

He cocked his head my way, studying my face. "Just bathing?"

"Well." I trailed my fingertip down his bare chest. "Maybe a bit more than just a bath if you're up for it."

"I'm always *up* for bathing, my mate."

His cock pressing against the inside of his loincloth proved it.

Stepping away from me, he held out his hand. Like always, he bristled with weapons straps, with long crystal blades spiking up from either side of his back, plus sheaths on his thighs and around his waist holding even more, though shorter blades. He was a walking arsenal, and frankly, I only had to look at my alien warrior to be turned on.

I took his hand, and he backed toward the cave entrance, tugging me along with him.

Inside, he lifted me and nudged me against the cold stone wall. It shocked me as much as his hot heat pressing against my front did, and I couldn't get enough. I wrapped my legs and arms around him and moaned, opening my mouth to deepen our kiss.

Our mouths still connected and with me wrapped around his body, Aizor stepped away from the wall and stumbled down the tunnel, diving into one of the first pools we came to. A glance out of the corner of my eyes showed we were alone, at least. I didn't think we'd used this pool before, but maybe we should make a plan to bathe our way through them all.

My snicker broke through the kiss, and he lifted his head, chuckling along with me even though he didn't know why I'd laughed.

"You, lovely Vanessa, are about to get a solid taste of your alien mate."

"I like the solid idea, as well as a taste."

He lowered me to my feet and quickly stripped me. His loincloth dropped to the ground, where it melted into the dirt, the gods absorbing it for cleaning. I'd even gotten somewhat used to that. No dirty clothing to trip over and no worrying about finding time to hang things out to dry.

We climbed into the pool and sank onto seats, both of us moaning about how amazing it felt. My skin was softer than it had ever been and . . . well, who could complain about natural lube? Especially with a guy as big as Aizor.

He attacked, pressing me against the surround.

I succumbed, climbing all over him again, urging his hands to roam my body just as his mouth devoured mine. He was addicting in a way I'd never anticipated. Pure, heady lust rippled through me. I'd never get enough.

His fingers slid between my legs, and I bucked against him, needing him fast and furious. I adored his gentleness, but right now, I wanted high heat and full charge ahead.

"Now," I growled the moment I came up for air.

"At your command, my lovely mate." He spun me around and jerked up my hips.

I braced myself against the side of the tub, groaning as he rubbed the head of his cock against me. He delved a little inside me, spreading the natural slippery stuff in the water.

And then he braced my hips and plunged inside, driving hard to seat himself fully.

We both groaned again.

He leaned over me, caging my body with his own, and started moving. Slowly at first, but as his second cock coiled around to latch onto my clit, he gave way. Like a flood rising after a violent storm, he was a wall that couldn't be denied.

"More, more, more," I snarled.

He laughed, but then his entire body shuddered, and he started moving faster, driving into me so hard my thighs butted against the stone surround.

I was on fire, and nothing was going to put out the blaze but this male. With each thrust, I released a sharp bark of pleasure. His growls joined in, and he went even faster.

And when his fingertips curled beneath me, finding my nipples and rolling them, I gave way, waves ripping through my body.

His shout of pleasure joined in, and he pumped even faster. Harder. Driving me into a second orgasm.

Only then did his pace slow. He kept moving gently after that while my body kept quivering, loving what came after as much as it had savored what came first.

The next morning, I woke in our fur bed to find him gone, but that wasn't unusual. Sometimes Aizor had meetings with various members of his clan. He'd finish and come back to me.

He'd always come back to me, and the knowledge thrilled through me.

I knew what I had to do. How should I tell him?

I left our crystal home, and spying Franklin scooting past the dining building and along a trail weaving into the woods, I hurried to the kitchen, requested a plate of food, and followed.

"Franklin," I called out as I entered the woods. I stopped, looking around, but I didn't see him. His usual whine didn't greet me either. "Where are you, little guy?" I walked farther down the path, calling out to him periodically.

The trail wove below the cliffs to the left of the circle of crystal homes, and I kept stopping to admire the spiky vegetation that bent at my touch yet felt and looked like solid glass. How long had the crystal aliens been on this planet? It must be thousands of years, since their structures were prevalent in everything I'd seen so far. It took a long time for a person to acclimate to eating glassy vegetation, so maybe we were talking about millions of years.

Would I ever learn more about their history? They were tightly woven into Zuldruxian society, to the point the people believed the crystals were gods. In many ways, they served that role well. They cared for the people and had a close-knit relationship with them. I wasn't one to discount anyone else's religion.

The ground dropped off considerably on my right, the edge of the path giving way to a steep, jagged cliff made up of boulders, scruffy trees, and rich, purple soil flecked with gold.

I hugged the inside of the trail as I walked.

"Franklin?" Finally, I came to a stop. "Where are you?"

His whine rang out ahead, and I hurried in that direction, rounding a curve in the path to find him sitting not far ahead.

I dropped to my heels and laid the plate on the ground.

He started forward but stopped suddenly, hissing.

Someone rushed up behind me and shoved my back.

I skidded across the path on my belly and toppled over the side of the cliff.

CHAPTER 32

AIZOR

"Have you seen Vanessa?" I asked Jessia. She sat with Trevar, Brulon, and their mother at a table in the dining area, eating lunch.

"No, I haven't." She looked around. "Is she in the kitchen? I think she said something about wanting to experiment with loosag-na earlier. Frankly, I was looking forward to trying it, but when I arrived to eat, she wasn't here. She may have decided to prepare the loosag-na a different day and slipped past us." Her indulgent smile took in the younglings. "These boys keep a person busy."

"They sure do," the younglings' mother said.

Vanessa wasn't in the kitchen, though Muzzire was.

"Have you seen my mate?"

He continued to eat a cookie, smacking his tusks with pleasure at the taste. "I have not." He held it out. "These . . . I've never had anything like them before. They're not bribard."

"They're not." Leaving him to finish his cookie, I

went to our home. Everything appeared tidy, and for the first time ever, I didn't like how efficient the gods were about cleaning. If things were lying about, it might give me a clue as to where my mate had gone.

Outside, I scanned the area.

Krute came over to stand with me. "I found evidence that Nevarn's males came close to our homes again early this morning." He scowled toward the thick woods surrounding our small valley. "Not only that, but I found more big footprints. I tell you; others are intruding into our lands. We need to attack them all. I've been saying this for a long time. I understand why you hesitate." He laid a hand on my shoulder. "You have a new mate. She's lovely. But we must protect our people."

"You're right." I wasn't sure how to do it, however. I didn't want to endanger my mate or the clan. "I don't want to start a war. We're too few already. Neither clan can afford to lose anyone." As for the large footprints, I needed to study them myself before deciding about that.

"I understand this. I do." Krute shook his head. "But we must do *something*."

"I'd like to call a clan traedor gathering."

"Like you did to plead with the gods for a mate?"

"Perhaps, if we talk about this, we can come to a decision that will avoid war."

"You know what Nevarn wants," he said.

"More land to spread out in. More hunting grounds."

"We can't give in to him. If nothing, you'll appear weak."

"I won't give in," I grumbled. "I'm not weak." The

last came out louder than I'd intended, loud enough that Jessia, walking with the younglings toward her home, paused and looked our way.

Stunned by my outburst, Krute backed away a few steps. Good. He needed to respect me as his traedor even when he didn't approve of my actions.

"I cannot act based on my feelings," I said in a more reasonable tone. "I must think of all of us. Would you like to see our younglings killed in battle?"

"Of course not."

Now, he sounded defensive, but he should.

"Yet here you are, urging me to lead an attack against another clan. Do you think they'll run, and we'll chase them all the way to the desert, and they'll remain there? Because I don't. Nevarn will stand, and he will fight. And we will lose males, as will his clan. If we lose too many, he'll give chase. He won't stop when he crosses into our territory. He'll come here. We could lose our homes and this village we've only recently settled. You know his clan doesn't live within the grace of the gods' exoskeletons like we do."

"I've heard they live in wooden homes. Can you imagine? They'll burn. Rot. Collapse on top of them while they sleep." He sighed. "However, I see what you mean. We don't want this. There must be a way to keep them from encroaching on our land."

"Which is why I'll consult with the other traedors. It's not weak to seek guidance. A strong leader listens before he acts."

"Alright. I'll give you time to speak with them."

I lifted my brow ridge. "*Give?*"

"I want to act. So do a few of the other males."

"You're talking of challenging me again."

"I don't want to." He spun on his heel and started walking away but turned back to face me. "But we can't allow this to continue as it is."

I was tempted to leap, to drag him down and show him once more that if nothing else, I possessed the strength needed to hold my position as traedor. But what purpose would that serve? He'd slink away once more, and next time, he might not come to me with his concerns; he'd do what he pleased behind my back.

After I located Vanessa, I may need to reconsider who should take the place as my second.

Because Krute may not be the best person for that job.

I awoke to someone carrying me and a throbbing pain in my left arm. It bled, blood trickling off my fingers and down my side. Thinking Aizor must be holding me, and I was safe, I snuggled into his embrace.

His scent was totally wrong. Looking up, I'd never seen this alien before in my life.

Squawking, I flailed, almost passing out when pain exploded in my arm. His grip on me tightened. He was so much larger than me that he barely had to use any of his considerable strength to make me hold still.

"Let me go," I snarled, tears trickling from my eyes. I wasn't scared, though I wasn't sure why, but my arm . . . It hung at an odd angle, telling me it was broken. Even worse, shattered bone gouged through my skin.

"I need a doctor. A hospital," I cried out. "I'm going to get gangrene. My arm will rot and fall off. I'm going to die." And I'd never see Aizor again, never feel his touch or hear him whispering sweet words in my ears.

"You won't die. I'll protect you, tiny one," the male said. He wore furs, unlike those in the Indigan Clan who dressed in clothing provided by their gods. "I found you lying on the ground, and you're sorely wounded. I'm taking you to my clan's healer."

"Take me back to the Indigan Clan. My mate . . ." Should I mention him, or would that only put him in danger?

"*Who* is your mate? Indigan, you say? That means you belong to Aizor." His head cocked as he strode along a path weaving through the woods. Other males dressed in a similar manner trotted along with him, bristling with simple weapons. I spied wooden spears, and one male held a large bow with a quiver full of arrows strapped to his spine. Feathers jutted up behind his head.

Otherwise, they looked much like Aizor's people, from their blue skin to their silver hair.

"I belong to myself." It seemed silly to protest about something like this when my arm was going to rot and fall off. "My clan has a healer. Please, take me to them. You'll be rewarded."

"Rewarded, you say?" The male carrying me laughed, a rich sound. He was handsome, as were all the Zuldruxians, but my heart belonged to Aizor. "I doubt anyone in the Indigan Clan will reward one such as me."

"You're Nevarn." The realization sunk into me, making me shake. Even this subtle movement made agony blast up my arm to my shoulder. My head pounded and spun, and I worried I'd pass out and be defenseless. "Please. Don't kidnap me. Take me back to my mate." I loved him. I'd already realized that. I was going to tell him tonight that I was staying here, that I didn't want to return to Earth.

If I didn't tell the gods on the island tomorrow, they'd automatically send me back.

"If you won't take me to the Indigan Clan, would you please take me to the island gods?" I asked. Maybe they'd help me after I told them I wanted to stay.

He frowned. With a leap, he jumped over a boulder blocking the path. The trail leveled off, telling me we'd reached the lower valley, and he picked up his pace to jog. "Why would you wish to go there?"

My arm jarred; it was all I could do to remain conscious. "Please, just do it." My vision swam and my arm throbbed.

His frown deepened. "Be quiet now. We're approaching my clan's territory, but there are beasts that—"

A roar echoed to our right.

The males jogging with us shared concerned looks and they started running, weaving through a forest filled with enormous trees like the ones growing in the western United States. Sequoia? Yes, that was what they were called.

Each of his steps made pain bolt through me. My vision wavered, and if he didn't stop, I was going to start screaming. I'd never stop. Giving way to the pain would draw the attention of whatever hunted the forest, so I kept my mouth shut. They couldn't run forever, and when they stopped, I was going to break free and flee toward the island. It was in this general area, and I'd find it. My arm was useless, but my legs still worked.

Please stay awake!

Stomps echoed in the woods. My heart slammed against my ribcage as if it, too, wanted to bolt. I sucked in deep breaths of air, panting through the agony.

"Put me down," I hissed. "Please."

"Here?" He shook his head. "Are you aware of the beast that hunts us?"

"My arm hurts so much," I whimpered.

"Which is why I'm taking you to our god. She'll heal you."

She? "Another crystal building?"

"Not crystal." He scoffed. "Our god of wood is superior to theirs."

"That's what they all say."

"Why would you run from me when I'm only trying to help? I've watched the Indigan Clan for days. I wanted to make sure you were treated right."

"It's not up to you to decide something like that."

"Of course it is. I'm male, and you're a foolish female. Are all of your kind like this?"

"I'm not foolish. You're the one snooping around my clan, spying on us."

He drew himself up stiffly. "I don't spy. I merely watch to make sure they don't do anything they shouldn't."

"Maybe pay attention to your own clan instead."

"My clansmales listen to me. I don't need to watch them."

Men. "Put me down."

"No."

"As you said, a beast is hunting us. I want to be on my feet to run."

"Will you run faster than me and for a longer distance with your injured arm?"

"I'll try."

His glare took in my legs. "You're puny. You have no muscle mass. One swipe of the beast's claws will send you flying into the side of a tree. You'll be dead before you hit the ground and become the creature's meal not long after."

"I hope the crystal gods never send you a mate. You're arrogant, conceited, and irritating."

He snorted. "Fortunately, my god doesn't listen to you."

We'd see about that.

"Hold your arm," he said. "Clamp your hand over the wound. Each drop of blood is a trail for the creature to follow."

My skin quivered, and I whimpered. I'd faced a horrifying beast when I arrived, and it sounded like another was on our trail, and I was leading it right to us.

"Run faster, then," I snapped, slapping my hand over the wound.

The world wavered. Only the stomp of his feet and the agony slamming through my arm kept me awake.

A roar rang out from our right.

"You're taking too long. It's getting closer!"

"It won't catch us."

"Climb a tree or something."

"They climb as well."

Well, wasn't that nice? "Then find some bushes to hide behind." We were out in the open, racing along a wide trail. The creature would see us from a mile away.

"How about this, puny female?" He ran faster, aiming for a huge dark purple tree with lighter lavender leaves that had to be as wide as a house.

"You're going to smack into it. Is that how you're going to save me?" *Crystal gods, please do something about these cocky males.*

Before he could impale us in the tree, the bark . . . parted. There was no other way to describe it. It split down the center, each side sweeping away like they were curtains at the start of a Broadway show.

He strode inside and the walls closed behind him, leaving me alone with him in utter darkness.

Franklin kept coming to me and whining. Assuming he was hungry, I gave him food.

I still couldn't locate Vanessa, not in the pools, our home, or in the dining area.

Where was she?

Finally, when Franklin wouldn't leave me alone, I stooped down and held out my fingers for him to sniff. "Do you want pats? Vanessa gives you lots of pats."

But Franklin only darted away, rushing toward a trail weaving into the woods. He stopped and looked back at me, whining again. I don't know why, but an uneasy feeling shot through me.

I followed Franklin. He raced ahead of me onto the trail, stopping to look back as if he hoped I'd remain with him. I spied the plate lying on the trail ahead and jogged over to it and stooped down, noting the food Vanessa often fed Franklin. After, I started examining the ground around it.

That's when I found evidence someone had fallen over the edge of the cliff.

With my heart on fire and fear bolting through me, I leaped, racing down the side at too fast a pace, bellowing my mate's name. Partway down the steep hill, I found evidence someone had laid in the grass. It was crushed in a small enough circle that I suspected this was where Vanessa lay after she'd fallen. It had to be her. Rising, I peered around. Where was she now?

I worked in widening circles, slowly, until I picked up tracks. Many had been here. And since the tracks leading away were deeper than what I might make, I suspected one of them was carrying a person.

Nevarn had taken my Vanessa.

I was going to kill him.

My eyes didn't have time to adjust to the dark before lights bloomed overhead. I peered up to find something glowing. Insects? No, the lights twisted through a vine. A plant then, perhaps. The light outlined a small room carved into the inside of the trunk. I took in smooth wooden walls, an equally smooth wooden floor, and an arched ceiling overhead.

"Come," the male said, lowering me to my feet but keeping a tight grip on my uninjured arm. "She's inside." His hand swept to a door I hadn't noticed, the seam blending into the far wall.

"We're inside a tree," I said.

"Very good observation, female."

"My name's Vanessa." I wouldn't share my name other than the fact that I hated being called *female*.

"As you said, I'm Nevarn."

"I've heard about you. You killed your mate." My skin peppered with goosebumps, and my arm throbbed. I wanted to rip out my hair and scream. "Are you going to kill me too?" At this point, I might welcome it if it meant I'd no longer feel the agony bolting up my arm.

"I didn't kill her, so you're safe—for now."

"You wouldn't happen to have pain pills on you, would you?"

"Come, silly female." He pretty much dragged me to the door, and it slid open just like the outer wall of the tree. When we passed through the opening, it closed behind us.

"How did you make the tree do that?" I asked.

"Our god does it for us."

Despite the agony, I was curious, peering around, taking in the walls that looked like they were made of wood, but I suspected was . . . "Is your tree made of crystal as well?"

"No, wood."

"But I thought everything was made of crystal."

"In the Indigan Clan, most of it is. You're with the Celedar Clan now." He banged his fist on the wall. "Our god is one of wood."

I nodded, but even this slight bit of movement made pain rocket through my head. It was all I could do to focus and not flop to the ground, curl into a ball, and weep.

"There are many gods in my world, not only the ones the other clans worship. Ours, however, are real." His chest puffed.

"That's what all the clans say."

"Yet, ours truly are real." He waved for me to go ahead of him, and since I wasn't convinced that his gods would let me out even if I beat on the wall, I decided to remain with him for now. I'd plead with the healer to release me.

We walked through a narrow tunnel that ended at yet another door that opened when we got near. The next room was much larger; the ceiling had to be three stories up. It was empty except for a tall, glassy chair with a person sitting on the smooth surface. She rose, equally tall and very slender, with limbs like the roots of a tree, her hair spiking up like spires on the top of a castle. Her face had a smooth flatness I found fascinating, and while she had eyes, they didn't blink, suggesting she had no eyelids. No nose either. A slash of a mouth without lips completed her face.

She glided across the room and floated around me, making almost no sound other than a subtle whisper. Her gown was blue on the bottom and gold on the top, exactly like the tree around us. Her dress didn't move or shift on her body, appearing fused to her form.

"You're injured," she said. Sort of said. I understood her, though she didn't speak with words like me or in my mind like the alien on the island. Her voice was a melody floating across my skin, sinking deep until I could under-stand her.

I should be afraid of a being like this. Her clan consid-ered her a god. And for the first time, I understood why. She was magnificent. But she didn't frighten me for some reason. "I fell. I'm in a lot of pain." My words came out in gasps. If I didn't sit down—lie down—soon, I was going to pass out.

"I can heal your arm. Will you allow me to help you?"

"At this point, I don't care what anyone does to me as long as my arm stops hurting."

Her arm lifted, separating away from the rest of her carved wooden body. She laid the end, what I'd call her hand, though she had no fingers, on my fractured arm.

Air hissed from my lungs as pain spiked through me. Before I could jerk away, the pain eased, followed by a low burn flashing up and down my arm.

Like someone hit a light switch, the agony went away.

Gasping, I gaped down at my arm. The bone no longer stuck through the skin and the skin had not only sealed closed, I didn't see a scar.

"You're . . . thank you," I said.

She dipped her head forward before turning and gliding back over to sit in the chair.

No, it was a throne, and she was a glorious queen.

"You're not Zuldruxian," she said, her voice tinkling through the air.

"I'm from Earth."

"I don't know of a place called Earth."

I advanced toward her. Should I be scared of her? Probably. While she might not be a god, she was from an alien race unlike any I could've imagined. A very advanced alien race. "Earth is a planet." I flicked my hand upward. "It's out there somewhere. I was stolen and brought here."

"I'm sorry."

"From what I can tell, you weren't involved."

"I was not."

Her head tilted, and she studied my face before her inky black gaze glided down my body. "Would you like to return to your Earth?"

"No." I lifted my voice. "No! I want to stay here. Please, if you can tell the other gods not to send me back, I'd be eternally grateful."

She stilled. "How grateful?"

I met her gaze with mine full of steel. "What would you like me to do?"

CHAPTER 36

AIZOR

My mate was bleeding. Someone was carrying her. I was going to rescue her.

And then I would kill whoever took her, lay waste to him until there was nothing left for the forest beasts to pick over.

I followed the trail of her blood splattered on the ground. How could such a tiny being lose so much blood and still live? My heart roared, my pulse pounding in my ears as I ran along the trail, only slowing to make sure they hadn't left the path and traveled in a different direction.

Nevarn had stolen Vanessa, and I would rip his arms from his shoulders, his legs from his hips and then, while he lay whimpering on the ground, I'd sever his head from his body.

This I vowed.

As I wove through the forest, I had to slow my pace. Enormous trees towered around me, so tall, it would take hours to climb them. Had he taken her up into the canopy? It wouldn't surprise me. Without crystal god exoskeletons, where did his clan live? Krute suggested in wooden structures, but if they remained on the ground, they'd be eaten.

As I rounded the backside of yet another tree, still following the trail of my mate's lifeblood, someone bellowed on my right and leaped toward me. He smacked into me, trying to drive me to the ground.

I swung out, the back of my fist impacting with his jaw. He shuddered but held his footing. Spinning, I kicked, and he took the blow in his belly, stumbling backward. Big and broad, he had to be at least a head taller than me. As huge as whoever had been spying on my clan from the mountain range above my village?

He snarled, gnashing his tusks, his eyes wide and feral. I'd never seen him before, and if someone had mentioned a male such as him, I didn't remember.

Did he belong to a clan I'd never heard of?

He grunted and rushed me, his head lowered like a battering ram.

I flung myself to the side, rolling and rising to my feet. As he roared and raced at me again, I slashed out with my crystal blades. He spun and twisted, evading each blow.

Renewing my efforts, I bellowed and spun, swinging my swords.

He slashed out with his arms, deflecting them. With a grunt, his hands snapped out, and he gripped the sharp side of my swords, holding tight even as I tried to wrench them free. Like I'd impaled them in the trunk of a tree, they remained fixed and unmoving.

He yanked, trying to take them from me. I'd survived three worthy challenges in my rise to traedor, but I'd never seen anything like this before.

"Let go or I'll cut you," I snarled.

He gnashed his tusks and renewed his efforts, wrangling with me for control of my blades.

I released one and grabbed a short blade from the sheath on my thigh. I swung it up, gouging the side of his belly deeply, aiming for a non-vital area.

I'd killed. Too many times. I hated the thought of taking the life of this mighty warrior even if he had been watching my clan.

"Relent and I won't hurt you again," I snarled. "We can talk. As traedor, I'd welcome you by my fire." Or try to as long as he stopped attempting to kill me.

He tipped his head back and bellowed before flinging my sword up and grabbing the hilt when it came tumbling down.

Before I could threaten him with my blade once more, he pivoted and bolted into the woods, taking one of my swords with him.

I stood on the forest floor, panting, wondering who he was and where he'd come from. If he'd wanted to kill me, he could've done so. Instead, he appeared to want my weapon more than to battle.

Was he a member of the Celedar Clan? Before I killed Nevarn for stealing my mate, I'd ask him.

Down one sword but surprisingly unscathed after

the battle with the enormous brute, I circled around to find the trail again and raced through the forest.

I ran across an open area leading directly to a large tree.

The trail ended at the smooth trunk.

Tipping my head back, I bellowed my mate's name.

CHAPTER 37
VANESSA

"I wish for . . . companionship," the carved god—goddess? –said.

"I'm not sure what you mean." I wavered, wanting to leave but feeling strangely compelled to remain here with this alien.

"I have no one to talk with," she said.

"But you live with this clan."

"They consider me a god. They don't speak with me very often."

That was sad. "What's your name?"

"I don't have a name."

"What do you mean?"

"My people don't . . . name each other."

"How do you refer to one of you who isn't there?" She truly was from another world. Or her ancestors were, assuming her species reproduced.

"We don't."

"I guess you don't *need* a name." I shouldn't feel bad

for her. Names didn't mean much. It wasn't like we picked them for ourselves. But . . . I guess without one she felt . . . generic. That wasn't the right word, but I couldn't think of a better one.

"If you were going to name me, what would it be?" she asked.

"Oh, I couldn't do anything like that."

"Why not?"

"Because . . ." I strode closer to her and lowered my voice to keep Nevarn from overhearing. "They think you're a god."

"And you don't."

"You aren't one. Right?"

She said nothing, just stared at me.

"You can't be a god."

"Why not?"

"Because . . ." I didn't have an answer.

"Not everything has an explanation," she said. "Go ahead. Name me."

"You should name yourself." I explained about how babies were born on Earth and given names—ones they might never choose for themselves. "Name yourself and you won't end up with everyone calling you Brunhilda."

"I don't wish to do this for myself, though Brunhilda . . ."

"Don't even go there."

"Then *name me*."

"What if you're insulted by my choice?"

"Name me!"

I jerked in a breath. "My mom's name was Helena."

"Helena." She said it slowly as if tasting it. "I like it. Thank you."

"You're, um, welcome."

Pounding erupted from outside, and we all looked that way.

"Her mate has come for her," Helena said, her lidless eyes turning toward the door before flicking to Nevarn hovering near the wall. "You need to release her."

Something slammed against the outer wall, and the entire tree shuddered.

Helena frowned. "He will harm this structure that has been here for many, many generations."

"Vanessa," Aizor bellowed.

"Aizor!" I raced to the door but couldn't find a way to open it. "Let me out of here." I looked back at Helena. "Thank you for healing my arm."

She dipped her head forward. "Come see me again."

"If I need healing?"

"For any reason, even to talk."

I couldn't imagine what she'd want to talk about, but why not? "Sure. Thanks for the invitation."

Nevarn thrust himself between me and the door. "You cannot leave."

"If you don't get out of my way, I'm going to kick you."

He scowled down at me. "What do you think a kick from a puny female like you will do?"

"Do you really want to find out?"

"You're insignificant. Much too small to cause harm. I doubt you could hurt a mighty warrior like me."

"This is your last chance to get out of the way," I snarled.

"You'd be wise to listen to her, Traedor Nevarn." Even I could hear the warning in Helena's voice.

"I'm not convinced she's his mate," he said, though patiently. He wasn't a horrible guy. Conceited, yes. But someone would love him one day—and put him in his place. I almost wished I could be here to see it and cheer that poor woman on.

"See this knee?" I lifted it and tapped it with the tip of my finger.

He nodded slowly. "I . . . do."

"*Males*," the carved wooden woman said behind me. "They never listen, do they?"

"You're damned straight, they don't," I said.

"Yes, damned straight," she quipped.

"We listen," he said, frowning at my foot as I dropped it to the floor.

I curled my finger for him to lower his head and spoke slowly. "If you don't get out of my way, I'm going to plant this knee in your groin, and you're going think about your life choices every time you take a step after that."

His face cleared, and his eyes widened. With a little catch in his throat, he eased to the side, revealing the door.

"Open it, if you please," I said.

He reached over and touched something, and the panel slid to the side.

"Thank you." Turning, I waved to Helena. "Thanks again for the healing. Do you enjoy coffee?"

"I don't know what coffee is," she said.

"Do you drink liquids?"

"Sometimes."

Good enough. "You'll love it. One day soon, I'll bring you coffee, and we can sit, have a few cups. We can share girl talk."

"I have never had . . . girl talk, either."

"Then you've been missing out."

Her tickling hum echoed in the room, and her body shook with her laughter. "I believe you're right."

CHAPTER 38
AIZOR

I rushed across the forest floor holding a long, thick tree trunk across my shoulder and slammed it forward, impacting it with the side of the tree. My mate was inside; this I knew. And I was going to destroy the tree to rescue her.

The tree shuddered but the slight seam of a door didn't budge.

Pivoting, I trotted some distance away again and turned, racing toward the tree once more, battering the door. I kept doing this, over and over, until sweat dripped down my face, my muscles screamed, and the trunk started falling apart. Undeterred, I ripped a new trunk from the ground and roared as I stomped toward the tree with it braced on my shoulder.

Before I could fling it toward the trunk, the center of the seam split, creating an opening.

My Vanessa, my glorious, beautiful mate, stepped outside with a smile on her face.

When she held out her arms, the trunk tumbled from my arms, landing on the ground with a heavy thud. I rushed toward her and swept her up, holding her close.

"Are you okay?" I asked.

"I'm fine. Perfectly fine."

Relief made my limbs tremble.

"No one is ever going to steal you from me again," I growled into her throat.

"You're my hero," she declared, kissing my face and my neck.

"Who do I need to kill? Name them, and I'll sever their head from their body and mount it in front of our home."

"Let's skip the head severing, let alone the mounting, okay?"

"How did you get here?"

"Nevarn brought me."

I snarled. "I'll kill him!" Glaring around and hefting my crystal sword, I tried to find him. "Nevarn? Come out, you coward. Show yourself so I can slice your belly wide open, stomp on your guts, then rip your arms from your shoulders."

Vanessa snorted. "Boy, when you go all in, you go all in. No ripping arms off people or slicing into bellies either."

"He harmed you."

"He didn't." She leaned back in my arms. "He didn't steal me."

That soothed my rage, though only somewhat. "What happened?"

"I was on the path, trying to lure Franklin close for treats when someone came up behind me. They pushed me, and I fell over the side of the cliff."

"I found tracks, signs of this. Did you see who did it?"

She shook her head. "No, but it wasn't Nevarn."

"Surely not one of my clan?"

"I don't know who it was."

"I'll track them down and rip off *their* head."

"And I'll cheer you on while you do it. Well, not rip off their head. But if it was someone in your clan, punishing them will be enough for me."

"You're too kind. Too gentle." I smacked my fist on my chest. "I'll handle this in the way I see best."

She sighed. "I understand what you're saying. I'm a pacifist, though I'm not squeamish. I might look away while you do it, however."

"You don't need to watch." I spun her around in my arms. "I'm glad I found you, mate."

"Me too." Her smile faded. "When I fell, I must've hit my head because the next thing I knew, I woke with a broken arm. A bone was sticking out and it was bleeding like a stuck . . . Okay, I'm going to scrub that image from my mind as soon as possible. The thing is, I was horribly injured and in incredible pain. Nevarn found me and brought me here where his god healed me."

"Nevarn helped you?"

"Strangely enough, yes. He said he and his clansmen have been spying on our village because they were afraid you'd kidnapped me, that I wasn't your mate." She rubbed her mark.

"I *will* kill him!"

"He now knows he's wrong, and I bet he won't encroach on Indigan territory again."

I grumbled. "Are you sure I can't rip off his head or at least one of his arms?"

"I'd rather you didn't. I'm friends with their god, and I don't believe she'd be happy if you did something like that. She might actually defend him."

"I don't wish to offend his god."

"Then let it go. When I return to visit Helena, I'll mention your concern about Nevarn. She'll speak with him, and I bet you anything, he and the members of his clan will leave us alone." She held out her arm, turning it this way and that. "It looks as good as new. We're going to have coffee together."

I lowered her feet to the forest floor but held onto her hands. I couldn't bear to let her out of touching distance. "You and Nevarn are going to have coffee?"

"Not him, the god, Helena and me. We're going to visit and have girl talk."

I couldn't understand much of what she said, though *god* stood out. "There are no crystal structures in this forest. No gods."

She tugged a hand away and patted the tree. "This is their version of a crystal structure. Nevarn's clan uses these trees for houses."

I peered up at the canopy that swayed in the breeze. Birds swooped about, and the chitter of a drettire echoed through the woods to my right.

"When I come back to have coffee with Helena, I'll

introduce you." Vanessa frowned. "But we have an urgent matter we need to take care of right away."

Pain arched through my chest like I'd taken a spear through the heart. I knew exactly what she meant. "If you plan to leave me, you don't need to go to the island gods. Remain here, and they'll take you."

"Can I . . ." She shook her head and gave me the sweetest smile. "That's the thing. I need to get there before they send me back. I'm staying with you, Aizor. I love you, and there's no place I'd rather be than by your side."

"Mate." I cupped her face and curled forward to kiss her. "Precious mate."

She looked toward the sky. "How long will it take for us to reach the island? I have to be there before sunset."

The sun hovered on the horizon. I swept her up again and pivoted, bolting toward the lake. "Hold on to me, mate, because I'm in love, which makes me the fastest male in the Zuldruxian world."

I would run forever if it meant Vanessa would remain with me.

CHAPTER 39
VANESSA

We reached the shore as the sun was slipping away. Aizor blew on the horn to call the giant puffer fish. I fretted while we waited. Would we be too late? I could almost feel the crystal aliens sucking me from Aizor's arms.

The lake creature breached on the shore, and I didn't hesitate before leaping inside its mouth.

Aizor held me in his arms as the beast swished back into the water and took us to the island. When the fish grounded itself on the opposite shore and stretched its mouth wide, Aizor bolted, splashing through the water and up onto dry land. He didn't stop but raced toward the central crystal compound with me in his arms.

We'd almost reached the front door when the sun slipped away.

An alien bristling with weapons stepped in front of us, brandishing his sword. It was so dark, and he was in shadows, I couldn't tell who he was.

"Muzzire," Aizor said in a dead tone, carefully lowering me to the ground and tucking me behind his big body. "Why?"

"We don't need mates like this. We have females," Muzzire cried out. "Don't go inside. Then the gods will send her away."

"I'm staying," I said. "We came here to tell them that."

"Then you'll die." With his weapon lifted, he leaped forward.

Aizor barreled into Muzzire, sending him flying back against the outside wall of the crystal building. Before he could follow up the blow with a slash of his blade, Muzzire was absorbed into the wall.

I gasped. Aizor strode closer and carefully touched the surface.

"Watch out," I cried, tugging him backward. "You could be pulled inside too."

"I've never seen anything like this before." He stooped down to examine that section of the wall. "It's as smooth as if he was never here, but we both saw him. Heard his traitorous words."

"He attacked me. All to avoid you and other traedors from mating with us."

"The gods have spoken."

I wasn't sure about that, but the one thing I did know was that we needed to get inside and speak to the crystal aliens before they sent me back to Earth.

Aizor straightened and took my hand. We hurried

inside the building and across the huge room to the one with flowers that would take me to the gods.

Inside, I jogged over and stood in the same spot I'd taken what seemed like ages ago. I'd grown since then.

And I'd fallen in love.

Would the crystal aliens believe me?

A blossom enveloped me and sucked me down. When I bottomed out, I waited, my heavy breathing the only sound echoing around me.

You've returned.

"Don't you dare send me back," I barked.

A low hum rang out, reminding me of Helena's laughter. Were these gods related to her or were they all different species?

You wish to remain with Aizor?

"Yes. I love him. I want to be with him always."

So, it shall be.

I was projected upward and when I spurted onto the floor, Aizor scooped me up and held me close.

"You're not returning to your planet," he said.

"I told you I love you, that I want to stay."

"Mate, you make me very happy." He gave me the sweetest kiss, but fire soon burned through it. When he lifted his head, he grinned. "The wall or the floor this time, my love?"

My smile joined with his. "I want to go home— to *our* home. And then we can do both."

CHAPTER 40
EPILOGUE
VANESSA

One Week Later

After breakfast, Aizor took my hand, and we left the dining area. "Would you like to see my shop? I still haven't had a chance to take you there."

"Yes, I have an idea for a game we could build if you have any scrap wood lying around."

"I have plenty."

We'd been busy over the last week, dealing with the aftereffect of Muzzire's treachery.

When we returned home, we found Muzzire lying in the central dining area on the floor, his arms and legs bound with vines.

The clan had gathered, and he had a chance to state his reasoning for his actions. Our clan was in complete agreement that he was wrong, that he had no right to try to harm me despite his concerns, that the gods had spoken, and their wishes needed to be respected. The last seemed to be the part that horrified many the most, though my new friends expressed grave concern for my safety and were glad to know he hadn't hurt me.

As traedor, it was part of Aizor's job to pronounce Muzzire's sentence: Banishment to the wasteland beyond the great forest. Krute would travel with him and make sure he didn't come back, though Muzzire had declared he welcomed the chance to redeem himself in the eyes of his gods. He wouldn't be allowed to return to the clan for a year and only then if he vowed to put aside his anger with the gods' plan for the Zuldruxians' future.

I couldn't wish him well, and I wasn't eager for his return, but I'd forgiven him for causing me pain.

Aizor and I walked down the hill and through the woods, though we took a different direction than the one leading to the meadow with the oven he'd built me. I planned to make dough this afternoon and tonight, we'd finally have pizza. I was starting simple, with only a cheese topping. I also had ideas for the smoked meat his clan had in abundance. It tasted a lot like brisket.

I'd bribed the crystal aliens to produce chips, and some of them had a nice corn flavor.

Nachos anyone?

We left the woods and took a trail weaving around the base of a stiff cliff. I hadn't traveled this way before.

Aizor stopped, frowning at the woods to our right.

"What are you looking at?" I asked, peering in that direction but not seeing anything. A memory of the abominable who'd nearly eaten me when I first arrived stomped through my mind, making my skin quiver.

"It's nothing." He led me farther along the cliff, still shooting speculative looks toward the woods.

I still didn't see anything, and the skin on the back of my neck crawled. "Should we go back?"

"I have a surprise for you at my shop."

"Okay but being ground to dust by the abominable would ruin your surprise."

He hefted his spear and grunted. "Do you think your mate can't defeat any foe we might face in the forest?"

"One of these days, you'll meet your match."

"I already have in you, my pretty mate." His smile made everything better. Hearing absolutely nothing in the woods sent my mood in a completely different direction. Maybe we could take a nap later today inside our home . . .

"Alright." I lifted my chin and tightened my spine. "Let's keep going." My nervousness gone; I started chattering. "Where do you find trees big enough for your projects?"

"They grow taller farther down the mountain. I drop them and ask Voolon to drag them to my shop."

"Is that where you mill the wood?" I explained what I meant, though I didn't know much about sawmills.

"Yes, that's what I do. The gods kindly gave me a mill to saw my wood like you describe."

How was it powered? I guessed I was about to find out.

At the end of the tall cliff, we entered the woods and walked downhill some more.

The path exited out into a big clearing full of tall, wavering grass, lots of little pink flowers, and a crystal building on the right side. Why had I thought his shop would be constructed from wood?

A metal monstrosity sat to one side of it; that must be his sawmill since a pile of logs had been stacked nearby.

We approached the squat blue glassy structure and went inside.

I stopped and gaped, taking in the wooden counters lining the outside walls, all of them covered with boxes, cooking tools, and things I couldn't identify in various stages of construction. "It looks like Santa's workshop."

"Who is this sinta?" Aizor asked, though with humor shining in his voice. I adored that he was never jealous. In fact, he encouraged me to interact with everyone in our clan, saying that my role as a traedor's mate was honored and revered, that I could give advice much like the gods. I wasn't sure about that, but I loved talking with everyone and finding out what they enjoyed eating. Now that Muzzire had been banished, I'd taken over some of the meal prep with Jessia's help. I adored crafting new dishes for everyone to try, and she begged for Earthling stories.

We did that, plus we played with the kids.

Would Aizor and I have a youngling one day? Perhaps. I wasn't in any rush. I adored the fact that it was just us, and I wasn't ready to leave that behind.

When I visited with Helena the day before, we not

only sipped coffee, but we also talked about this. She told me she'd spoken with the others of her kind and assured me that the other women and I were brought here to find true love with Zuldruxian mates, not to become brood-mares for the next generation. If we wanted children, we could have them. If we didn't, that was fine with her and the other aliens as well. All we needed to do was speak our wishes, and they'd provide some sort of birth control.

As for the woman with red hair I'd been worried about, Helena said I'd meet up with her again soon, that she'd found her true mate with a Zuldruxian male, and they'd travel to visit with our clan in a short time.

As for children, I'd decided to let fate give us a youngling or leave us happily without one.

"Would you like to see your surprise?" he asked, taking my hand and tugging me over to a large object covered with a cloth.

"What is it?" I danced beside him, giddy with excitement.

He ripped off the cloth. "*Fook eff!*"

I couldn't stop laughing, and my laughter soon gave way to tears. Then I had to remind him that I cried when I was either sad *or* happy, something he and the other Zuldruxians still found strange. Maybe if some of the other women joined our clan and did the same thing, they'd finally understand.

Because his gift was gorgeous, I didn't laugh for long. I kept crying as I sat in the chair he'd made for me; one I could place near the fire. It was big enough for him to sit with me or the boys when I told them a story.

"Do you like it?" He fretted with his tusks, rubbing them across his upper lip.

"I love it." I stroked my palms along the smooth arms. "How did you find time to make it?"

"I came here when you were asleep," he said gravely. "I wanted you to have something special, something from my heart."

"Aizor." This male kept breaking me and putting me back together again. "I love you."

He leaned forward and kissed me with enough heat to tinder the fire simmering deep inside. We'd definitely need to take a nap soon.

"What did you hope to do with the wood scraps?" He waved to a box full of pieces in all sorts of sizes.

"Jenga."

"Jenga?"

"It's a game. Can we bring the box of wood up near the fire?"

"To burn?"

"Never. We're going to stack it and then tug out pieces from different sections of the pile."

"And you'll find this fun?"

"Won't you?"

"I'll carry it up there tonight."

Because I couldn't resist looking, I slid off the chair, admiring it again, before I walked around his shop, tracing my fingertip across various things he had either finished or was still working on. "What do you hope to do with all these wonderful items?"

"Give them away."

"You could sell them at a clan gathering." The first would be held in one month.

"I'd rather gift them to whoever wants them."

"See? That's just like Santa. You're my big blue, alien Santa."

He picked me up and carried me back to my new chair where he sat and settled me on his lap, his arms enfolding me. I wrapped my legs around him and grinned up at him.

"Is Santa sexy times?" he asked.

This was a phrase I'd shared with him. He'd used it for almost everything, even when it came nowhere close to applying. Last night, he'd declared the ice cream I'd made was sexy times. Although, when he drizzled some of his melted desert on my chest and proceeded to lick it off, I had to agree.

"Santa's very sexy times," I said.

"Good. Because that's me." He pointed at his chest. "Many sexy times."

Maybe it was my own special kink, but I'd always had the hots for Santa.

My smile widened. "There's only one thing you need to do if you want to be the best *fook effing* Santa."

He gazed at me quite solemnly. "What is it? I live to please you, my mate."

My grin turned sly. "During sex, would you shout ho-ho-ho?"

CHAPTER 41

EPILOGUE 2
AIZOR

Today, all the clans would gather on the gods' island to celebrate new life and savor spending time together. Everyone in my clan would attend. A gathering hadn't been held in so long, even Jessia didn't remember when.

Before we left, I played with Franklin—now renamed Frankie—on our bed. She'd delivered four kits, and they were adorable. They were just beginning to crawl, and I swore they knew when I held them, because they purred just like Frankie did when she lay beside us on our furs at night.

"Are you almost ready to leave?" Vanessa asked, entering our home. She stroked my shoulder.

"Yes." I snuggled one of the kits against my neck.

"That one's Helena's."

Once they'd matured and Frankie had weaned them, they would go to their new homes within our village—other than one promised to Helena.

"How can you tell them apart?" I asked.

Vanessa shrugged. "They have distinctive differences."

I couldn't see it, but this was just one more wonderful thing about my mate. She treated everyone as if they were unique and special—including me.

Rising, I kissed her, and we left, traveling on Voolon to the shore of the lake with the rest of our clan.

My people would all travel in caipareels to the island, each and every one of them. No one wanted to miss this glorious event.

Leaving the caipareel on the opposite side, I carried Vanessa up onto the shore, returning to the water to allow the tiny creatures to clean the caipareel sluice off my legs and feet.

She shook her head when I returned to her. "This still freaks me out, but it's kind of amazing."

I didn't know what freaking out was, but as long as she gave me a pretty smile, I didn't care if the sky was purple, and the trees had turned green. Her love was all that mattered.

As we walked toward the central god structure, we nearly ran into Nevarn on the path, arriving with his clansmales, all fifteen of them. There wasn't a single female among them, but it wasn't as if my clan had many either.

"What are you doing here?" I asked him, still fuming that he'd taken my mate, let alone spied on us. I appreciated that he'd begged his god to heal her, but he should've brought her to my village, not his own. And he never should've questioned the gods giving Vanessa to me.

"My former traedor told me that my clan could attend the gathering." His gaze traveled to Vanessa, and he subtly turned, lifting his thigh as if he needed to protect his groin. "It's been three years. I'm no longer banished."

I grunted. "Then you're rejoining your former clan?"

"We have our own clan, our own lands." He stiffened his spine. "I'm traedor, and we will remain where we are. And . . ." He grumbled; his gaze fixed on my mate. "I apologize for spying on your clan. We promise to remain within our own lands from now on unless you invite us to visit."

I wanted to snarl at him, to shout that he had no right to spy at all, but I also liked the idea of a secure border on his side.

And from the way Krute was nodding slowly and looking at me with an apology in his eyes, I knew letting this go would work out best for both of our clans.

"You're welcome at my fire," I said.

"Thank you," Nevarn said quite solemnly. "I'll bring . . . Helena. She would like to speak with your kitchen god. She mentioned something about cookies."

"Your god is also welcome."

Vanessa just grinned and leaned into my side.

I could respect a male who chose to lead rather than follow. If his former traedor, Firion, had forgiven Nevarn, how could I do anything less? As if thinking of them made them appear, members of the Dastalon, or sky warrior clan, appeared overhead, soaring their mighty crystal beasts in a circle like birds of prey before guiding them down to land a short distance from us.

"Whoa," Vanessa said, cringing into my side.

I placed an arm around her back, holding her close "Their beasts won't cause you harm, my mate. Nor will this clan. They're friends. Come, I'll introduce you."

She shot me a wide-eyed look I'd become used to. She wasn't familiar with our world yet, but she was slowly learning about not only the Indigan Clan but the other Zuldruxians I was friendly with.

We left Nevarn and strolled over to where the Dastalon Clan had landed their beasts. They unharnessed them and left them to graze, striding confidently toward us.

Firion was as tall and broad as me, and about my age. He wore dark blades in sheaths at his sides, and when the wind swept across the island, it whipped his hair around his pretty face. Would my mate find him attractive? I shouldn't feel jealous, but . . . every female I'd known swooned when they saw Firion, even Jessia.

"This is Firion, the traedor of the Dastalon Clan," I said gruffly, waving to the other male when we stopped on the path, facing each other. "Firion, this is my mate, Vanessa, who you will not smile at."

Firion smiled. "Why not?"

Vanessa's breath caught, and she held out her hand to the other male.

He stared at it before stooping down and sniffing it. "Lovely."

"*My* lovely," I growled.

"Of course." He flashed his tusks.

Vanessa limped into my side, stroking her hand across my abdomen exposed by my formal, adorned vest. I'd asked the gods to dress me to impress the other traedors, and they'd delivered glorious clothing unlike any I'd worn before. Vanessa also looked amazing, wearing a tunic with intricate embroidery that hung to her knees and was belted with a sash as blue as our crystal homes.

"It's nice to meet you, Firion." Vanessa grinned up at me. "My mate is amazing, don't you think?"

And maybe I didn't feel jealous after all. I took her hand, squeezing it, and she squeezed right back.

"*Fook eff*," I told Firion, turning and guiding my mate toward the central building.

Firion snorted and walked behind us with his males, entering the building but walking to the right rather than following us farther.

"He's cute," Vanessa said. "Not as cute as you, but cute." Her mood sobered when she saw the pods holding her fellow Earthlings—the term she'd shared with me. "They're all still lying there. I want them freed. They should be able to pick their own mate, not be given to a male they've never met," Vanessa said. "Helena and I were just saying we thought this was wrong." She stared past me, her eyes lighting up.

I turned to find "Helena" striding across the room, her limbs thudding against the floor with each step. The first time I'd seen her, I'd dropped to my knees. She'd laughed, then she told me to stand and look her in the eye, stating she wasn't like the others.

She was a god come to life, and I'd praised her, worshipping her in the manner I'd found worked best with those of her kind.

She went on to explain that she was the same yet different from the others, that she didn't need me groveling before her, that she preferred I treated her as a friend.

I couldn't imagine how that was possible—though I tried.

Vanessa rushed over to Helena, tipping her head back to gaze at her friend. "Fix this."

"How should I fix . . . this?" Helena asked.

"Tell the other gods to free the women."

Helena frowned and appeared to stare inward. Finally, she shook her head. "They have refused. I can't do anything about this, though I agree. It doesn't seem fair."

Vanessa growled and stamped her foot, and I was glad her snarls were not directed at me. "I'm going to fix this, I swear."

Helena placed a restraining arm on my mate's shoulder. "Trust them in this. They mean no harm to your friends."

After sucking in breaths and shoving them out, Vanessa huffed. "For now."

"Yes, for now. I'm asking you to remain patient and trust that they know what's best."

Her lips thinned before she forced a smile. "I'll accept it for now."

"Excellent." Helena peered around the room. "I believe it's time to party, is it not?"

A term she must've learned from my mate.

"Yes, it is," Vanessa said, though sadly. "Let's join the others." She held out her hand, and we returned to where everyone had started to gather.

As we mingled, my mate meeting one Zuldruxian after another, her smile grew stronger.

That was when I caught movement near the opening to the vast chamber.

The enormous warrior I'd battled in the woods stood in the opening with my crystal sword sheathed at his side. He gazed wistfully at us before his chest lifted and released. Turning, he strode back outside.

Why didn't he stride inside like every other traedor and join us? Because I knew he had to be a leader. There was no way that male would ever follow another.

"What are you looking at?" Vanessa asked, squeezing my hand. Her gaze followed mine, but the male no longer haunted the doorway.

"It's nothing," I said.

Or was he?

With a shrug, I lifted my mate and kissed her. Things would sort out with the other male one day; I knew this.

I kissed my mate again.

Vanessa wrapped her arms around my shoulders and gave me the prettiest smile. "What was that for?"

"It was to show you I love you."

She kissed my nose before pressing her forehead into mine. "And that, my wonderful mate, was to show you that *I* love *you*."

I shrugged off all thoughts of the other male and carried Vanessa over to join the crowd. It was time to celebrate. I'd found my true mate.

And soon, other males would find their true mates as well. My people would flourish.

And the gods would once again thrive.

I hope you enjoyed Vanessa & Aizor's romance
and your introduction to the Zuldruxian world!

Next is Xax's story.
Can he and a red-headed woman from
Earth find true love together?
Pick up your copy of
Treasured by the Alien Rogue

Find Ava's books on Amazon and her website,
avarosswrites(dot)com.

TREASURED BY THE ALIEN ROGUE

Stolen from Earth, I was sent to a distant planet to become the bride of a big blue alien. Do I dare let this gruff guy inside my heart?

Amanda: With my boss out to kill me, I run, only to be abducted by robocops. They knock me out and the next thing I know, a tiny pod I'm riding in crashes into a purple lake and a loincloth-wearing alien with lots of muscles, tusks, and a sardonic smile rescues me. Xax takes me home to his clan and announces I'm his new mate. There goes my dream of opening a tea shop in a cute little coastal Earth town.

But between building me a tea shop and protecting me from every scary thing that comes near, I'm finding Xax hard to resist.

Xax: Our plant god has gifted me with a mate, and I'm going to do all I can to satisfy her in every way possible. I'll pluck leaves in the forest to make tea. I'll call vines to construct a structure to house her new business. And I'll happily kiss her toes.

Can I convince Amanda to remain on Zuldrux as my bride?

Treasured by the Alien Rogue is Book 2 in the Brides of the Zuldrux Warriors Series. Expect humor, size difference, a devoted alien warrior who'd die to protect his fated mate, steamy romance, and an alien world you'll want to live in.

Consent and HEA guaranteed.

Get Treasured by the Alien Rogue now!

ABOUT THE AUTHOR

Ava Ross is a two-time *USA Today* Bestselling author who has written numerous titles, all of them featuring sweet and steamy romance. She fell for men with unusual features when she first watched Star Wars, where alien creatures have gone mainstream. She lives in New England with her husband (who is sadly not an alien, though he is still cute in his own way), her kids, and a few assorted pets.

ALSO BY AVA ROSS

Find Ava's books on Amazon and her website, avarosswrites(dot)com.

* 9 7 9 8 8 6 9 3 6 4 1 3 5 *